CHOOSING THE BRIDE

A tale of many improbable events

This is a work of fiction. All of the characters, organizations, and events portrayed in this novel are either products of the author's imagination or are used fictitiously.

Cover by Eugene Ivanov

Published by Dragonwell Publishing
(www.dragonwellpublishing.com)

ISBN 978-1-940076-46-1

FOREWORD

Ernst Theodor Amadeus Hoffmann (1776-1822) is known to the world primarily as the author of The Nutcracker, a Christmas tale immortalized as a famous classical ballet. It is less known that E. T. A. Hoffmann is also a pioneer of magic realism, whose works influenced generations of speculative fiction authors. Born Ernst Theodor Wilhelm, Hoffman changed his middle name to Amadeus as a tribute to his favorite composer, Wolfgang Amadeus Mozart.

E. T. A. Hoffmann's tales heralded major discoveries of the modern days, and are considered among the major influences in literature and culture.

"Choosing the Bride", a novella written at the break of the 19th century, predicted the existence of e-reader – a small volume one can always carry in a pocket, which could turn into any book you want. Like other discoveries foretold by speculative fiction authors, people dreamed of making this one a reality for a long time, until it finally found its way into ordinary households and has become an essential part of our lives.

Step into the mythical world of Hoffmann's old Berlin, and experience the enchantment of his magical tale...

CHAPTER 1

which tells about brides, weddings, chancery clerks, tournaments, witch trials, sorcerers, and other entertaining topics

On the night of the autumnal equinox, Herr Tussmann, a clerk in the privy chancery, was returning to his home on Spandauerstrasse from a coffee shop where he had the habit of spending an hour or two every evening. Herr Tussmann prided himself on being precise and regular in everything he did. He always took off his coat and boots while the clocks on the bell towers of St. Mary's and St. Nicholas's churches struck eleven, so that with the last stroke of the clock he could stick his feet into his roomy slippers and pull his nightcap over his ears.

It was almost eleven, and Tussmann was in a hurry (in fact, he had to proceed almost at a run). He had just turned out of Kenigstrasse into Spandauerstrasse, when loud knocking at the street corner froze him to the spot.

A tall, wiry man wrapped in a dark cloak stood at the bottom of the old town hall tower, rapping on the door of Herr Warnatz's, the ironmonger's shop. When he received no reply, the odd stranger stepped back and sighed deeply, looking up at the windows of the tower above.

"My dear sir," Tussmann said politely. "You seem to be knocking on a wrong door. This tower is completely abandoned. No one lives there, except for rats, mice, and several owls. If you wish to purchase something from Herr Warnatz's impressive hardware collection, I suggest you to come back tomorrow."

"Respected Herr Tussmann – " the stranger began.

"Chancery clerk, for a number of years by now," Tussmann pointed out, somewhat surprised that the stranger seemed to know him by name.

The stranger did not appear to mind the interruption as he went on:

"Respected Herr Tussmann, you are mistaken regarding my intentions. I am not here to purchase any hardware, nor do I have any interest in Herr Warnatz. This is the night of the autumnal equinox, and I am here to see the bride. I am certain that my passionate sighs and knocking have reached her ear, so she is about to show up in that window above."

The man's solemn voice echoed so hollowly through the empty street that Tussmann felt an icy shudder run down his spine. The first stroke of eleven rang down from the bell tower of St. Mary's, and at this very moment he heard clattering and rustling above and a woman's figure appeared in the tower window.

As the bright light of the street lamps fell on her face, Tussmann gasped. "Oh, my God! Heavens above – *what* is this?"

The clocks rang through eleven strokes – the time when Tussmann was supposed to be putting on his nightcap and slippers. At the last stroke, the female figure vanished.

For a moment, Tussmann completely lost his senses. He sighed and groaned as he stared up at the window, and whispered: "Tussmann! Tussmann! Chancery clerk, remember yourself. Don't let yourself get confused by the Devil."

"You seem to be troubled by what you have seen, my dear Herr Tussmann," the stranger said. "I only wanted to see the bride. You act as if you've seen something else altogether."

"Please, please," Tussmann said, "I would be so much obliged if you would be good enough to address me by my title. I am a chancery clerk, and truly, at this moment, a greatly perturbed chancery clerk – in fact, one almost out of his senses. I beg you, with all due respect, my very dear sir (though I regret that I am unable to address you by your proper title, as I have not the honor to be in the least acquainted with you, having never met you before – however, I shall address you as 'herr privy councilor', there are such an extraordinary number of gentlemen here in Berlin bearing this title that one can scarcely be in error in applying it) – I beg you, therefore, Herr Privy Councilor, to be so very kind as to tell me what kind of a bride were you intending to behold here at this hour of the night."

"You're a curious fellow," the stranger said. "So set on titles. I suppose, as a man who knows a number of secrets and mysteries and can give good counsel, I can go by the title of a privy councilor. I am surprised, however, that a gentleman such as yourself, so well versed in ancient writings and curious manuscripts, doesn't know that when an informed person – *informed*, if you understand what I mean – knocks on this door, or at least on the wall of this tower, at precisely eleven o'clock on the night of the autumnal equinox, he will behold, up in that window, the girl who is to be the happiest and luckiest bride in Berlin before the spring equinox comes around."

"Herr Privy Councilor," Tussmann exclaimed. "Most respected Herr Privy Councilor, is this really the case?"

"It is," said the stranger. "But we should perhaps continue our conversation somewhere other than the street? I believe you've already missed your usual bed time, Herr Tussmann, so why don't we head directly to the new wine shop in Alexanderplatz. Once there, I would be delighted to tell you more about this young lady, and anything else you wish to know. I hope my stories would help you recover your peace of mind, which something – I have no idea what – has disturbed so tremendously."

Herr Tussmann was a very moderate person. The only indulgence he ever allowed himself was to spend an hour or two every evening in a coffee shop, where he read newspapers and political pamphlets, or studied the books he brought with him, over a mug of good beer. He seldom touched wine, except after the service on Sundays, when he normally visited a bar and allowed himself a small glass of Malaga with a biscuit. To go to a wine shop at night was not normally an idea he would ever entertain. With this knowledge, it seemed odd that he followed the stranger toward Alexanderplatz without a word of objection.

The wine shop was empty except for a single customer, sitting by himself at a table with a big glass of Rhine wine before him. His deeply wrinkled face betrayed his advanced age. He had sharp, piercing eyes, and wore a long beard, fashioned in the tradition of those practicing the old faith, and the kind of clothes that used to be in style around 1720. Perhaps it was this peculiar clothing that made him look like an old relic coming from the past.

Now that Tussman had a chance to take

a better look at his companion, he had to admit that the mysterious stranger who invited him here, looked no less unusual. Tall, lean, and muscular, he seemed to be about forty or so. His face might once have passed for handsome. Dark eyes shone with youthful vigor from underneath his thick black eyebrows, complemented by a tall forehead, strong aquiline nose, finely sculpted lips, and a prominent chin. His coat and trousers were styled in the latest fashion, even though his collar, cloak, and a beret cap belonged to the later part of the sixteenth century.

However, it wasn't the clothing that made him stand out from any other man Tussmann knew. Perhaps it was the mysterious gleam in his eyes, or the hollow tone of his voice, but the overall impression was positively eerie.

As they approached the table, Tussmann's companion nodded to the old man sitting at the table, as if they were old acquaintances.

"Here you are again, after all this time. How do you feel? Alive and kicking, eh?"

"Just as you see," the old man growled. "Sound and healthy, always around at the right time and ready to act if anything's up."

"We'll see about that," Tussmann's

companion said, laughing. “We shall see.” He beckoned the waiter and ordered a bottle of the oldest claret in the cellar.

“My good Herr Privy Councilor,” Tussmann began.

But his new acquaintance immediately interrupted him. “Let’s drop the titles, my dear Herr Tussmann, once and for all. I am no privy councilor or a chancery clerk, I am merely an artist who works in noble metals and precious jewels, and my name is Leonhard.”

“Oh, so you are a goldsmith, a jeweler,” Tussmann murmured. He should have noticed earlier that the stranger could not possibly be a privy councilor. Antique mantle, collar, and beret were not the kind of attire privy councilors normally favored nowadays.

Leonhard and Tussmann sat down at the old man’s table, just as he watched them with a sour look. The claret arrived, and Tussmann, at Leonhard’s insistence, drank several glasses of the full-bodied wine.

Soon his normally pale cheeks began to glow as he sat at the table, looking into the distance and chuckling to himself, as if lost in the pleasant realm of his imagination.

“And now,” Leonhard said, “tell me openly and candidly, Herr Tussmann, why were you acting so strangely when you saw the bride appear in the tower window, and what is on your mind right now? You and I are very old acquaintances, whether you remember it or not; and as for this old gentleman here – you need no ceremony with him."

"Oh, heavens," Tussmann said. "Oh, good heavens, most respected Herr Professor – I do beg you to allow me to address you by this title; I am sure you are a most celebrated artist, and quite in a position to be a professor in the Academy of Arts – and so, most respected Herr Professor, how can I hide from you? I want you to know that I am, as they say, in a position of a suitor, and I am seriously thinking of bringing the happiest of brides home around the vernal equinox. It was rather startling, when you, respected Herr Professor, were so very kind as to let me see the fortunate bride to be."

"What?" the old man broke in. "Are you thinking of marrying? At your old age, with your appalling looks? Why, you're as ugly as a baboon."

Tussmann was so shaken by this that he could not think of anything to say.

"Never mind him," Leonhard said. "He means no offense, no matter what he sounds like. Frankly, I have to agree that it is a little too late in life for you to be thinking about marriage. You must be what, around fifty, are you?"

"I will be forty-eight," Tussmann said irritably, "on the ninth of next October – St. Dionysius's day."

"Well," said Leonhard. "It isn't only your age that's against you. You've always been leading a simple, solitary existence. You have no knowledge or experience with women. Can you imagine what could become of you in their hands?"

"Dear Herr Professor, you must really take me for a most foolish and inconsiderate person if you think I am going to plunge into matrimony without any counsel or reflection or advice. I weigh, consider, and reflect upon every step most maturely. Would anyone preparing for a difficult examination not be careful to study all the subjects on which he is to be tested? I see my marriage as an examination, for which I have prepared myself. I feel pretty certain that I shall pass it admirably – with honors. Look here, at this little book, which I always carry around in my pocket, studying it constantly ever since the time when I've made up my mind to fall in love and get married. Look at it, my dear sir; and you will be convinced that I am setting about this business in the most thorough and fundamental manner possible, and that I shall certainly not be found ignorant; although, as you say (and as I must admit), the feminine sex is – so far, and up to the present date – a complete *terra incognita* to me."

With these words Tussmann pulled a little book in parchment binding out of his pocket, and turned up to its title page, which read:

A Brief Tractate on Diplomatic Acumen.

A guide book on how to develop one's political sense and proper conduct to hold oneself appropriately in any society.

This creation by Herr Thomasius, translated from Latin, is an essential read for anyone who deems oneself wise, or wishes to become wiser.

Includes a complete index.

Frankfurt and Leipzig.
Published by Johann Grossen and Sons, 1710.

"Now, let me quote you," said Tussmann with a smile, "what this worthy author says in section six of chapter seven, which is dedicated entirely to the subjects of wedlock, and the wisdom of the father of a family and the master of a household:

"'*My first advice: do not hurry. It is much more sensible to marry at a mature age, when a man is wizened with life experience. Only loose and unfocused people enter into an early marriage, thus wasting their physical and mental strength. A man in his middle years is, of course, not a youngster, but youth ends only when the years advance.*'

"And then, with regard to the choice of the object of one's affections and matrimonial pursuits, the amazing Herr Thomasius says, in the ninth section:

"'*In all your choices, stick to the golden mean. My advice: do not settle your choice on a woman too beautiful or too plain, too rich or too poor, too noble or too low-born. Seek out the one whose social standing is similar to your own, and stick to the middle in regard to all of her other qualities.*'

"This is what I have always guided myself by. And (as directed by Herr Thomasius in section seventeen), not only did I have a number of conversations with the lady of my choice, but I did so with the knowledge that it is easy to be deceived by hiding one's faults during casual interactions. Thus, I have taken opportunities to have *frequent* interviews with her; frequent interviews make it very difficult for people to conceal themselves from one another, don't you see?"

"My dear Herr Tussmann," the goldsmith said, "it appears to me that such interviews with women, or whatever you please to call them, require a great deal of experience, unless you want to open yourself to a possibility of being made a fool of."

"Even in this," said Tussmann, "the insightful Herr Thomasius comes to my aid, with ample instructions on how to converse with ladies in the most meaningful and courteous manner, even how and when to introduce the due amount of playfulness and wit, suitable for the occasion. In his fifth chapter, though, he points out that one ought to use moderation in using these means, just like a cook must be moderate in the use of salt. Pointed speech should never be employed as a weapon, but used only in defense – just as a hedgehog uses its spines. In addition, a sensible person must always watch not only their words but also their facial expressions, for they betray those thoughts we choose not to express verbally. In the end, it is our behavior, rather than words, that tends to awaken liking or disliking."

"I see," the goldsmith said, "there is no getting around your arguments. You are closed up in armor of proof. I bet that you have already gained the affections of the lady of your choice by means of those wonderfully deep diplomatic dodges."

Tussmann lowered his eyes modestly. "I strive to direct all my endeavors – following Thomasius's advice – to attain a deferential, though kindly, demeanor. I strive to invoke love and mutual admiration by setting an example – just like a yawn can instantly trigger yawning in an entire company. But, reverentially as I follow these instructions, I am also sconsius about not going go too far. I always remember that – as Thomasius says – women are neither angels nor demons, but mere human beings; and, they are in fact, weaker than men in both mind and body – which, of course, is fully accounted for by the diversity between the sexes."

"Look at you," the old man said, "sitting here chattering nonsense without a stop; spoiling the good hour in which I hoped to enjoy myself after all the hard work I've been going through."

"Hold your tongue, old man," the goldsmith said. "You ought to be thankful that we are putting up with you. I can tell you your company is anything but pleasant. Your manners are abominable. You ought to be kicked out of decent society. Don't let the old man disturb you, dear Herr Tussmann.

You believe in the old times; you're fond of old Thomasius. I go a good deal further back. What I care about is the time to which, as you see, my dress partly belongs. Aye, my good friend, those were the days. In fact, the small miracle you've observed tonight in the window of the town hall tower comes from the magic of these good old days."

"I don't quite understand you, Herr Professor," Tussmann said.

"Well," said the goldsmith, "there used to be splendid weddings in those days in the town hall – very different from the weddings nowadays. Plenty of happy brides used to look out of those tower windows. Let me tell you, Berlin was a very different place back then; nowadays everything is marked with the same stamp of tediousness and boredom, so prevalent that people are forced to find pleasure in this boredom itself.

"In those days there were entertainments, feasts, very different from anything we can see now. Let me tell you about a grand reception thrown by the citizen of Koln in 1581 to honor the arrival of the Kurfürst Augustus of Saxony, with his wife and his son Christian. A hundred noblemen rode out to meet them, while the citizen of Berlin, Koln, and Spandau, lined both sides of the road from the gate to the palace. Next day there was a splendid joust at the ring, at which the Kurfürst himself, as well as Count Jost of Barby appeared. The nobles wore fine suits with gold embroidery and tall golden helms, their shoulder, knee and elbow pads fashioned as golden lion heads. The rest of their bodies, clade in flesh-colored silk, made it seem as if they were naked, like heathen warriors in old paintings.

"There were singers and musicians hidden inside a gilt Noah's Ark, and on top of it sat a little boy dressed as a Cupid, in flesh-colored silk tights, with his eyes bandaged. Two other boys, dressed as doves in white ostrich feathers, with golden eyes and beaks, pulled the ark along; and when the prince ran at the ring and succeeded, the music in the ark played, and pigeons flew out of it. One of them flapped its wings and sang a most delightful Italian *aria*, and did it much better than our Court singer Bernard Pasquino Grosso from Mantua did seventy years afterwards (but not as charmingly as our prima donna sings nowadays).

"Then there was a foot tourney, to which the Kurfürst and the Count sailed in a large boat, covered with black and yellow cloth with a sail of gold taffeta; and behind His Highness sat the little boy who had been the Cupid the day before in a long coat of many colors, a peaked black and yellow hat, and a long grey beard. The singers and musicians were dressed the same way; and around the boat noble gentlemen from good families danced and jumped, wearing heads and tails of salmons, herrings, and fishes of other sorts: most delightful to behold. In the evening, around ten, there was a grand display of fireworks shaped as a large fortress manned by landsknechts, and the master-gunners played all sorts of pranks to amuse the crowds. Thousands of fiery stars shot into the sky – fiery horses, men, strange birds, and exotic beasts. The fireworks went on for more than two hours."

While the goldsmith was talking, the chancery clerk felt more and more excited, gulping down glass after glass of the wine.

"My dearest Professor," he exclaimed at last, in falsetto. "My dearest, most respected Herr Professor! What an amazing story – and so realistic. It sounds as if you've been there and seen it all yourself."

"Well," the goldsmith said, "what makes you think I haven't?"

Tussmann, who didn't in the least understand this question, was just about to ask for clarification, when the old man lifted his head and said:

"Don't forget the other kinds of grand

celebrations the citizen of Berlin enjoyed so much in those times you are praising so much. The New Market Plaza smoked with pyres, the streets ran red with the blood of innocent victims, forced under horrible torture to confess to whatever their twisted executioners came up with. Don't, I merely say, forget to tell your friend all about them."

"Yes, yes," Tussmann said. "Of course you mean the terrible witchcraft trials which took place in those old days. Ah. They were atrocious indeed; fortunately nothing like this happens anymore."

The goldsmith cast a strange look at the old man and at Tussmann, and said with a mysterious smile.

"Have you ever heard about the coiner Lippold, and what happened to him in 1572?"

Tussmann didn't have time to answer. But it appeared that the goldsmith didn't expect him to, as he went on:

"This coiner, Lippold, was accused of imposture and roguery. He had, at one time, been in the full confidence of the Kurfürst, and was at the head of all the affairs of the mints and the coinage in the country; always ready to produce large sums of money, no matter how large, when required. Whether because he was clever with words, or because he had some powers at his command that enabled him to clear himself of all blame in the Kurfürst's eyes – wash himself with the water from a silver basin, as they used to say, – he was about to be freed. But as the decision was being made, he was still kept under guard by the town watch, in his little house in Stralauerstrasse. And it so happened that he had an argument with his wife, who shouted in anger: 'If our gracious lord the Kurfürst only knew what a villain you are, and what atrocities you manage to commit by the help of that magic book of yours, you'd be in your coffin long ago!' The guards overheard this and reported to the Kurfürst, who ordered a careful search of Lippold's house. The magic book was found, and, when it was examined by those who understood it, Lippold's guilt was clearly established. He had been practicing magical arts to give him power over the Kurfürst, and to enable him to rule the whole country; only Kurfürst's piety enabled him to withstand those spells.

"Lippold was burned in the marketplace. When the fire was consuming his body and the magic book, a huge mouse ran out from under the scaffold and leaped into the fire. Many believed this was the demon who had been helping Lippold in his devilish deeds."

While the goldsmith was speaking, the old man sat leaning his arms on the table, covering his eyes, groaning and sighing as if suffering unendurable torture. Tussmann, on the other hand, did not pay much attention to the goldsmith's story. He was in good humor, and his mind was full of other thoughts. When the goldsmith finished talking, he asked, with a smile:

"Tell me, dear Herr Professor, was this young lady I saw in the tower window really Fraulein Albertina Fosswinkel? Was she truly the one looking down on us with her beautiful eyes?"

"What?" the goldsmith demanded. "What business have *you* with Fraulein Albertina Fosswinkel?"

"My dear sir," said Tussmann. "Good gracious, my dear friend, she is the very lady whom I have made up my mind to marry."

"Good God, sir!" the goldsmith cried, with a face as red as a furnace, and eyes glaring with anger. "You must be out of your mind. *You*, an old, worn-out pedant, to think of marrying that beautiful young creature! *You*, who, with all your erudition, and your 'diplomatic acumen,' taken from the idiotic treatise of that old goose Thomasius, can't see a quarter of an inch before your own nose. I advise you to forget about this, or you might find that you stand a good chance of having your wretched neck wrung on this very night."

The chancery clerk was taken aback. He was normally a quiet, peaceful man, incapable of saying a harsh word to anybody, even when attacked. But what the goldsmith had said was just too insulting. And then, Tussmann had drunk far more wine than he was accustomed to. With all this, it was perhaps no wonder that he did what he had never done before in his life. He jumped up to his feet and yelled out, right into the goldsmith's face:

"What the Devil are you saying, Herr Goldsmith? How dare you talk to me in this sort of way? You seem to be trying to make a fool of me. I presume from your reaction that you have the audacity to be paying visits to Fraulein Fosswinkel yourself. You think I don't know how your so-called magical vision at the tower was concocted? You've gotten her portrait somehow, and projected it onto the town hall window using a magic-lantern held under your cloak. My good sir, *I* know something about these things. You're going the wrong way about it if you think you're going to frighten and bully *me* by your cheap tricks."

"Be careful what you're talking about,"

the goldsmith said very quietly, with a strange smile. “Be very careful, Herr Tussmann. You are messing with the wrong people.”

And as he spoke, instead of the goldsmith’s face, Tussmann saw a horrid-looking fox’s snout, snarling from underneath the goldsmith’s beret.

The chancery clerk fell back into his chair.

The old man, though, did not seem to be in the least surprised by this transformation. Rather, he had suddenly lost his ill-temper altogether. He laughed, and said,

“Look at him, doing tricks and jests like no other. But these are nothing but cheap hoaxes that would never bring you to anything good. I know better ones. I can do things you haven’t dreamed about, Leonhard.”

“Let us see,” said the goldsmith, who had assumed his human appearance again. “Let us see what you can do.”

The old man took out a large black radish, trimmed it with his pocket knife, shredded it into thin strips, and laid them out on the table. Then he struck each of them a blow with his clenched fist. When they sprung up, one by one, they turned into gold coins, which he threw across to the goldsmith. But as soon as the goldsmith caught each of those coins, it turned into dust, raining down in a shower of crackling sparks. This infuriated the old man. He went on striking the radish shavings into gold pieces faster and faster, hitting them harder and harder, and they crackled away in the goldsmith's hand with fierier and fierier sparks.

Tussmann was nearly out of his senses with fear. At last, he pulled himself together and said, in a trembling voice: "Really, it's getting rather late. I'm afraid I must respectfully bid you both good evening." And, grasping his hat and stick, he bolted out of the room as quickly as he could.

When he reached the street, he heard his two mysterious companions burst into laughter. Its sound made the blood run cold in his veins.

CHAPTER 2

where a cigar that would not light up led to a love affair between a lady and gentleman, even though they had previously knocked their heads together.

Young artist Edmund Lehsen met the mysterious goldsmith Leonhard under somewhat more ordinary circumstances.

One day, Edmund was painting a beautiful group of trees in a lonely part of the Thiergarten, when Leonhard came up, and, without any ceremony, looked over his shoulder at the sketch. Edmund did his best not to react as he went on with his work, until the goldsmith said –

"This is a most extraordinary picture, young man. You are not painting trees, you are painting something else altogether."

"Did you notice anything unusual, sir?" Edmund said, beaming.

"I see all sorts of ever-changing forms and shapes peeping out from among those leaves: geniuses, strange animals, maidens, flowers. Yet the whole thing looks like a group of trees, with the rays of the evening sun streaming through them."

"Sir," Edmund exclaimed. "Either you have a special gift to see the essence of the matter, or I have been fortunate in successfully portraying my deepest feelings. Do you ever experience this feeling when, looking at nature, you see wonderful shapes and forms peering at you from the trees and bushes? That was the feeling I was trying to represent in this sketch, and I see I have succeeded."

"I understand," Leonhard said. "You wanted to take a break from your academic studies, to rest and relax by unleashing your imagination in the pleasantries of nature."

"Not at all," Edmund answered. "I

consider the process of painting one the best ways to study. A landscape painter is like a poet – or he has to be, if he wants to amount to anything in life."

"Dear God," said the goldsmith. "So you, my dear Edmund Lehsen, are going to – "

"Do you know me, sir?" Edmund said.

"Why shouldn't I?" said Leonhard. "I first made your acquaintance on an occasion which you, probably, don't remember much about; that is to say, when you were born. Incidentally, I must tell you that you've been behaving very well at the time, considering. You've given your mamma very little trouble as soon as you came into the world. Your papa was so pleased that he hopped about the room on one leg, singing *'The manly heart with love o'erflowing,'* from Mozart's Magic Flute.

"He handed you over to me, and asked me to draw your horoscope, which I did. Afterward I often came to your father's house, and you seemed to enjoy all the little bags of almonds and raisins I used to bring you. When you were about six or eight, I went away on my peregrinations, and when I got back to Berlin, I was glad to learn that your father sent you here from Münchberg to study the noble art of painting. The art collection in your native town can scarcely compare with those in Rome, Florence, or Dresden; or perhaps even with what Berlin will one day become, if all the antiques fished out of the Tiber, can be brought here."

"Heavens!" Edmund cried. "I do remember you now. You are Herr Leonhard, are you not?"

"Certainly," Leonhard answered. "Leonhard is my name. I must say I am astonished that you remember me after such a long time."

"I do," Edmund said. "I was always happy when you came, because you always brought me delicious things to eat, and played with me. I always viewed you with a mixture of awe and reverence. But what makes me remember you even more has to do with what my father used to say about you. He told us that your friendship was the most important one in his life, because you got him out of a number of troubles. And he used to tell us about your deep and mysterious knowledge of science, your ability to control secret powers of nature. In fact – begging your pardon for saying so – he often told us that you were none other than Agaspherus the Wanderer."

"Why not the Pied Piper of Hamelin? Or the King of the Kobolds?" said the goldsmith. "I suppose there is some truth to the notion that I did some good turns to your papa by means of my secret knowledge, or art as I tend to think of it. He was particularly pleased with the horoscope I've cast for you at your birth."

"The horoscope wasn't so very clear, though," Edmund said, blushing. "My father often told me that according to your predictions I should be a great something – either a great artist, or a great fool. In any case, I have to thank your horoscope for my father's consent to my wish to become a painter. Do you think everything you foretold is going to turn out true?"

"Oh, most certainly," the goldsmith answered. "There can be no doubt about that. At this moment you are on a straight path to becoming a great fool."

"What?" Edmund exclaimed. "How can you – "

"It is entirely up to you," the goldsmith said, "to avoid this fate and become a great artist instead. Your drawings and sketches show that you have a rich and lively imagination, the power of expression, and a great deal of skill in execution. If you manage to keep away from all the modern exaggerations and eccentricities and apply yourself to serious study, you might turn out to be good indeed. I congratulate you on your efforts to imitate the earnest simplicity of the old German masters. But, even with all this promise, you need profound intelligence, and a mind strong enough to resist the influence of the modern school, to wholly grasp the true spirit of the old German masters, and to penetrate completely into the significance of their pictures. Without these qualifications, the true spark will never kindle in your artist's heart, nor would you achieve the genuine inspiration to produce works which, without being imitations, shall be worthy of a better age. Nowadays young fellows think that when they patch together something on a Biblical subject, with figures all skin and bone, faces a yard long, stiff angular draperies, a perspective all askew, they have painted a work in the style of the great old German masters. Dead-minded imitators of that description are like a country lad who hides his face behind his hat during the church prayer and pretends that he can follow the song, or at least hum along with the tune."

The goldsmith went on to say much more about the art of painting, and gave Edmund many valuable hints and tips. Much impressed, Edmund asked how it had been possible for Leonhard to acquire so much knowledge on the subject without being an artist himself; and why he went on living in such seclusion, and never allowed his influence to bear on artistic efforts of all descriptions.

"I have told you already," the goldsmith said, "that my ways of looking at life, and at things in general, have been rendered exceptionally acute by a long – aye, a marvelously long – course of experience. Wherever I appear, I tend to produce a rather extraordinary effect – not only because of my nature in general, but because of the powers I possess. In fact, living quietly in Berlin is not so easy for me. I keep thinking of a certain person who might have been an ancestor of mine: so similar to me in so many ways that at times I almost believe that I am that person. I am referring to the Swiss by the name of Leonhard Turnhäuser zum Thurm, who used to reside at the court of the Kurfürst Johann Georg in 1582.

"In those days, every chemist was known as an alchemist, and every astronomer was called an astrologer; so Turnhäuser was very probably both. It is certain, at all events, that he did most wonderful things, and besides was also a skilled healer. Unfortunately, he also had a flaw: he wanted everyone to know about his superiority, he tended to get involved in too many affairs. This made him envied, even hated, the same way a rich man can spawn envy and hatred by showing off his wealth. Thus it came about that one day the Kurfürst received a report that Turnhäuser could make gold. Somehow, though, when asked to demonstrate this ability, he refused – perhaps because in truth he actually couldn't do it. And then his enemies said to the Kurfürst – 'See what a cunning, shameless rascal he is. He boasts of powers he does not possess, and carries on sorceries for which he ought to be burned at the stake like the old coiner Lippold.'

"This envy, hatred, and calumny brought matters so far that Turnhäuser had to secretly leave Berlin, to escape the fate similar to Lippold's. He went to Saxony, where he worked as a goldsmith, though he never gave up the study and practice of his science."

Edmund was amazed with the old goldsmith, who not only criticized the modern school, but also told Edmund secrets concerning the preparation of colors known to the old masters. Thus, the two men formed one of those perfect relationships that come about when a promising young disciple meets the affectionate paternal friendship of a teacher.

About the time this happened, one fine

summer evening, Herr Melchior Fosswinkel, a commission councilor, was sitting in the "Court Hunter" café inside the Thiergarten, having terrible trouble lighting up any of his cigars. They must have been rolled up too tightly. He was feeling more and more annoyed as he threw them down, one after another, until he exclaimed:

"Oh, God! Did I spend all this effort and expense to order my cigars directly from Hamburg to have all my pleasure spoiled? How can a man possibly enjoy the beauty of nature, or take part in any sort of rational conversation, when these damnable things won't light up? This is so upsetting!"

He had unintentionally addressed these remarks to Edmund Lehsen, who happened to be standing nearby smoking a cigar.

Edmund had not the slightest idea who the commission councilor was, but he immediately took out his cigar case and offered it politely to the desperate person, saying that he could vouch for both the quality and the drawing powers of his cigars, although he had not gotten them from Hamburg, but out of a shop in Frederichstrasse.

The commission councilor accepted, with a "Much obliged, I'm sure." And indeed, the cigar drew delightfully. As he sent out the loveliest clouds of blue fragrant smoke, he exclaimed:

"Oh, my dear sir! You have rescued me from the profoundest depths of misery. Do please accept a thousand thanks. In fact, I would venture to ask you to let me have one more of those magnificent cigars of yours, to be going on with when this one is finished."

Edmund assured the commission councilor that the contents of his cigar case was quite at the gentleman's disposal; and then they went on their separate ways.

Later on, at twilight, and Edmund was making his way out of the restaurant, navigating between tables and chairs with an idea of a new painting in his head, the commission councilor appeared in front of him and invited him to come and sit at his table. Edmund was about to decline, but just then he caught sight of a young lady – the embodiment of beauty, youth, and grace – seated at the commission councilor's table.

"My daughter, Albertina," the commission councilor said to Edmund, who was staring at the lady, so dumbfounded that he nearly forgot to bow to her.

He had seen her before – at the latest art exhibition, where he had found her admiring one of his own pictures. Not only that – she was describing the painting to an old lady and two girls accompanying her, explaining the features of the drawing and the grouping as if she knew a great deal about art. Edmund had been standing close behind her, drinking in the praise that flowed from her beautiful lips. He could not bring himself to go forward and say he was the painter, but when Albertina happened to drop one of her gloves, Edmund rushed to pick it up. As Albertina did the same, their heads banged together with a loud crash.

"Oh, good gracious!" Albertina had cried, clasping her hand to her forehead.

Edmund drew back, stepping straight on the old lady's pug. The poor creature yelped loudly, forcing him to stumble away, trampling the gouty toe of a professor, who screamed and devoted poor Edmund to all the infernal deities. People came hurrying from the neighboring rooms, fixing their lorgnettes upon Edmund. Shamed, he rushed out of the place amid the whimpers of the dog, the curses of the professor, the objurgations of the old lady, and the tittering and laughter of the girls, while several ladies took out their essence bottles and offered them to Albertina so that she could rub the essence into the big lump rapidly swelling on her forehead.

Edmund had barely admitted to himself

that during this disastrous encounter he had fallen deeply in love. Only the painful sense of his own stupidity prevented him from searching for Albertina all over town. He pictured her with a great red lump on her forehead, anger on her face, and bitter reproach on her lips, yet he still couldn't stop thinking about her.

There was not the faintest trace of either of these things, however, as he saw her now. When his father introduced Edmund, she blushed – very prettily – and said with a delightful smile, that she must be much mistaken if he were not Herr Lehsen, the celebrated painter, whose works she so immensely admired.

Those words ran through Edmund's nerves like an electric shock. He was about to burst into flowers of rhetorics, but at that moment the commission councilor clasped Edmund to his breast and said, "My dear sir, what about the cigar you promised me?" And while he was lighting the said cigar at the ashes of the former one, he said, "So you are a painter? And a great one, from what my daughter Albertina tells me – and she knows what she is talking about in such matters, I can assure you. I'm very glad you are. I love pictures, and, as my daughter Albertina says, 'art' altogether, most tremendously. I simply adore it. And I know something about it, too. I'm a first-rate judge of a picture. Tell me, my dear painter, tell me without hesitation, wasn't it you who painted those pictures which I stop and look at every day as I pass them, because I cannot help admiring the colors?"

Edmund did not quite understand how the commission councilor managed to see any of his pictures daily in passing, given that he had never painted any sign boards that he could remember. But after a good deal of questioning, it turned out that Melchior Fosswinkel meant a set of lacquered trays, fireplace screens, and other household objects displayed in a window of Herr Stobvasser's shop at Unter den Linden. Herr Fosswinkel indeed passed by every day around eleven in the morning, after his usual breakfast of four sardines and a glass of Dantziger at the Sala Tarone. These productions constituted his highest ideal of art. Worse, Fosswinkel's incessant chatter was preventing Edmund from making any approach to the young lady. At last, Fosswinkel's acquaintance came up to the table and engaged the commission councilor in a conversation, allowing Edmund a chance to sit down beside Albertina, who seemed to be pleased at this.

Everyone who knows Fraulein Albertina Fosswinkel is aware that she is not only the very personification of youth, beauty, and grace, but also, as a proper Berlin lady, dresses in the best taste in the latest fashions, sings in Zelter's choir, takes piano lessons from Herr Lauska, dances most gracefully, has sent a tulip charmingly embroidered and surrounded by violets to the a craft exhibition, and though by nature of a bright and lively temperament, is quite capable of displaying the proper amount of sentimentality required at tea-parties and other social events. Everyone also knows that she copies poetry and famous quotes from Goethe, Jean Paul, and other talented men and women, in the loveliest handwriting, into an elegant little book with a gilt morocco cover, and that in doing so she never makes any grammatical errors.

Of course it was natural that, sitting beside the young painter, whose heart was beaming with affection, she appeared several degrees more sentimental than was usual on the tea and reading-aloud occasions; and she lisped in the prettiest manner about such subjects as poetic feelings, depth of ideas, childlike simplicity, and so forth.

The evening breeze carried a waft of fragrance from the night flowers. Two nightingales started a lovely duet among the thick foliage overhead.

Albertina began, quoting from Fouqué:

"A rustling, whisper'd singing
Breaks through the leaves of spring,
And over heart, and sense, and soul
A web of love doth fling."

And Edmund, less timid now that the twilight was falling more deeply, took her hand and laid it on his heart, while he went on, continuing the quotation:

"Did I, in whispered music, sing
What my heart hears – aright –
From that sweet lay would burst, in fire,
Love's own Eternal Light."

Albertina withdrew her hand, but only to take off her glove, and then gave the hand back to the lucky young man.

He was just going to kiss it fervently, when the commission councilor broke in:

"Oh! I say! It's getting chilly. I wish I had brought my overcoat. Put on your shawl, Tiny. It's a fine Turkish shawl, my dear painter – cost fifty ducats. Wrap yourself up, Tiny; we must be getting home. Good-bye, my dear sir."

Struck by inspiration, Edmund immediately took out his cigar case and offered the commission councilor a third Havannah.

"I am excessively obliged to you," the commission councilor said. "You are most kind." He went up to the lamp to light the cigar, and Edmund took advantage of his absence to whisper to Albertina that he hoped she would let him walk her home. She put her arm in his, and Fosswinkel, when he joined them, seemed to think it natural that Edmund was going to walk with them all the way to town.

Anyone who has once been young, and in love – or who is both now at this present time (there are many who have never been either the one or the other) – will understand how Edmund felt at Albertina's side. Holding her arm, he felt as if he was soaring over the tops of the trees, up in the clouds, rather than walking along the park.

Rosalind, in Shakespeare's "As You Like It", says that the marks of a man in love are "a lean cheek, a bleary eye and sunken, an unquestionable spirit, a beard neglected, hose ungartered, bonnet unhanded, sleeve unbuttoned, shoe untied, and everything demonstrating a careless desolation." But those marks were as little seen in Edmund as in Orlando. Like the latter, however, who marred all the trees of the forest by carving his mistress's name on them, hung odes on the whitethorns, and elegies on the bramble-bushes, Edmund spoiled quantities of paper, parchment, canvas and colors, praising his beloved in horrible verses, and drawing her portraits without ever succeeding to achieve any likeness to the original. Added to the unmistakable somnambulistic look of a lovesick, and a befitting amount of sighing at all times and seasons, it was no wonder that the old goldsmith immediately recognized his young friend's condition.

"Hmmm," he said; "you don't seem to think what an inappropriate thing it is to fall in love with a girl who is already engaged. For Albertina Fosswinkel's hand is already promised to Herr Tussmann, the chancery clerk."

This terrible piece of news sent Edmund into the wildest despair.

Leonhard waited patiently till the first paroxysm was past, and then asked if he really wanted to marry Albertina. Edmund declared that was the dearest wish of his heart, and implored the goldsmith to help him as much as he could to remove Tussmann from his path and win the lady for himself.

The goldsmith pointed out that while a young artist may fall in love as much as he liked, to marry right away was a very bad idea. These were the kind of considerations that prompted young Sternbald to forgo marriage, and, for all Leonhard knew, to remain a bachelor up to this day.

This thrust took effect, because Tieck's 'Sternbald' was Edmund's favorite book, and he would have been only too glad to have been the hero of that tale himself. So he put on a pitiful face, and was very near bursting into tears.

"Well," said the goldsmith, "whatever happens, I can promise you that I will take Tussmann out of your way. It will be your job, however, to get invited into Fosswinkel's house and earn Albertina's affections. As for my operations against the chancery clerk, they can't begin till the night of the autumnal equinox."

The manner in which he approached this task is already known to the reader from the previous chapter.

CHAPTER 3

providing a more complete description of the chancery clerk, and explaining the reasons that prompted him to dismount the Kurfürst's horse, as well as other curious topics

From everything we have already learned about Herr Tussmann, it is already possible to vividly imagine his character and his habits. Still, to add to the description of his looks, it may be useful to mention that he was short of stature, bald, a little bow-legged, and prone to a most original manner of dress. His coat had extremely long tails and was styled in a fashion likely worn by his great-grandfather. His waistcoat was also of enormous length, as well as his trousers – not to mention his shoes that clattered to announce his arrival as loudly as the boots of a courier. It should be noted also that he never walked along the streets with regular steps, but jumped and bounced at a half-run, so fast that the long tails of his coat flew behind him like wings. Although there was something excessively comic about his face, his kindly smile made it pleasant to look at; although people tended to laugh at his pedantry and awkwardness, everyone liked him.

Tussmann's passion was reading. When he left the house, his coat pockets were usually crammed full of books. He read wherever he was, and in all circumstances; walking or standing, in church, or in a coffee shop. He read everything that came to his hands, but only old books – he hated everything modern. Today he would be sitting in a coffee shop with an algebra textbook; tomorrow he would absorb himself in a tome of Frederick Wilhelm I Cavalry Regulations, before moving on to "Ten speeches revealing Cicero's true nature as a pettifogger and a windbag", the 1720 edition.

Moreover, Tussmann was gifted with a most extraordinary memory. He had the habit of marking the passages which particularly struck him in a book, then read all those marked passages over again, after which he never forgot them anymore. Thus, he was known as a walking encyclopædia, and people turned to him for all kinds of historical and scientific references. And if, by any chance, he found any difficulty in supplying the required information, he would rummage through all the libraries and then emerge with the answer, greatly delighted.

Remarkably, when he was reading and to all appearance completely absorbed in a book, he also had the ability to hear everything that was being said around him. Quite often he would insert a highly appropriate remark into a conversation, or laugh at a joke without looking up from his book.

Commission councilor Fosswinkel and Tussmann had gone to school together at the Grey Friars, and they were close friends since those days. Tussmann had watched Albertina grow up. On her twelfth birthday, he had presented her with a fragrant bouquet, tastefully assembled by the finest florist in Berlin, and kissed her hand with the courtesy and gallantry no one would have imagined him to be capable of. Since that day the commission councilor had an idea to arrange Albertina's marriage to his old school friend. He thought this would be the least troublesome match, not to mention that Tussmann would be unlikely to request a high dowry. Fosswinkel hated putting himself into any trouble, was cautious of making new acquaintances, and, in his capacity as a commission councilor, tended to engage in excessive monetary calculations. On Albertina's eighteenth birthday he revealed this plan to Tussmann.

At first, the chancery clerk was terrified. The idea of entering the matrimonial estate, particularly with such a young lady who was also an amazing beauty, did not sit well with him. But over time he got used to the idea, and when one day Albertina, at her father's insistence, presented him with a coin purse she made from the most beautifully selected colorful silk, addressing him as "dear Herr Chancery Clerk" as she did so, his heart ignited with love for the charming maiden. He secretly informed the commission councilor that he was ready to marry Albertina, and as Fosswinkel immediately embraced him as his son-in-law, he considered himself engaged to her. Of course, he should probably have given some thought to the fact that the young lady herself had no idea whatsoever about this arrangement.

The morning after the strange nighttime adventure at the town hall tower and in the wine shop on Alexanderplatz, the pale-faced Tussmann burst into his friend Fosswinkel's bedroom. The commission councilor was very alarmed. Tussmann had never visited him at such an hour, and his manner and appearance clearly indicated that something terrible was going on.

"What, in the name of Heaven, is the matter with you?" Fosswinkel demanded. "Where have you been? What have you been up to? You look positively awful."

Tussmann did not respond as he collapsed into an armchair. It took several minutes before he was able to speak in a whimpering voice:

"Fosswinkel. Here, as you see me, in these clothes, with 'Thomasius on Diplomatic Acumen' in my pocket, I come straight here from Spandauerstrasse, where I have been running up and down ever since the clock struck twelve last night. I have not set a foot in my own house, or seen the sight of a bed, nor have I closed an eye for the whole night."

And he told the commission councilor all that had happened to him from the time when he first came across the mysterious goldsmith, till he made his escape from the wine shop as fast as he could, in his terror at the sorcery which was going on there.

"Tussmann, old fellow," said Fosswinkel, "I see you've been drinking. You are not used to wine, especially long after you ought to have been asleep; no wonder you had a lot of funny dreams."

"You are mistaken," Tussmann said. "You think I was asleep and dreaming? You think I don't know anything about sleep and dreams? I can explain to you what sleep really is, according to of Rudow's 'Theory of Sleep', and prove to you that people can sleep without dreaming at all; and as for what dreaming is, you will know as well as I do, if you read the 'Somnium Scipionis,' and Artimidorus's great work on dreams, and the Frankfort Dreambook; but, you see, you never read *anything* and that's why you are always making such rushed judgments."

"Now, my dear old man," the commission councilor replied, "don't you go and get yourself into a state of excitement. I can see, easily enough how you may have allowed yourself to be convinced to drink a bit too much last night, and then somehow found yourself in inappropriate company of men who got the better of you when they saw you drunk. But what I cannot make out is, why, in all the earth, when you escaped the place, didn't you go straight home to your bed, like a reasonable man? Whatever did you go wandering about the streets for?"

"Oh, Fosswinkel!" wailed Tussmann. "My old friend, my comrade from the Grey Friars. Don't you go and insult me by insinuations of that sort. Let me tell you that the infernal, diabolical enchantment practiced on me did not really go into effect until I got *into* the street. For, when I made my way to the town hall, every one of its windows was blazing with light, and there was music inside – a brass band, playing ballroom music. I am not sure how it happened, but, though I'm not a particularly tall man, I stood on tiptoes and was able to see through the window. And *what* did I see? – Oh, gracious powers of Heaven! *whom* did I see? *Your daughter*, Fraulein Albertina Fosswinkel, dressed as a bride, and waltzing like the very deuce (if I may permit myself such an expression) with a young gentleman! I knocked on the window and called out to her: 'Dearest Fraulein Fosswinkel, what are you doing here, at this time of the night?' But just then, some scoundrel walking down Kenigstrasse pulled off both of my legs, tucked them under his arm, and ran away, laughing. And I, the poor chancery clerk fell down straight into the mud, and started shouting: 'Watchman! Police! Stop the thief! – stop him! – he's got both my legs!'

"Just then, all the lights in the town hall suddenly went out, and my voice died away in the air. I was getting desperate, when the thief suddenly came back, and, as he flew by me like a mad creature, threw my legs back to me, right into my face. I picked myself up and ran to Spandauerstrasse. But when I got to my own door (with my key in my hand), there was *I* – *I*, myself, standing there already, staring at *me*, with the same big black eyes which you see at this moment. I stumbled back in terror, right into a man standing behind me, who seized me into his strong grip. By the halberd he was carrying, I thought he was the watchman; so I said, 'Dearest watchman! – my good man! – please drive away that wraith of chancery clerk Tussmann from that door there, so that *I*, the *real* Tussmann, may get into my house.' But the man growled out, 'Why, Tussmann! You're surely out of your senses!' in a hollow voice; and I saw it wasn't the watchman at all, but that terrible goldsmith. Terror seized me and I said: 'Most respected Herr

Professor, pray do not take it ill that I should have thought you were the watchman, in the dark. Oh, Heavens! Call me whatever you choose; call me in the most uncourteous manner 'Tussmann,' without a title at all; or even 'My dear fellow!' I will overlook anything. Only please, I beg you, rid me of this terrible enchantment. 'Tussmann!' he said, in that awful hollow voice of his, 'you shall be left in peace, if you swear to me, right here on this spot, to give up all idea of marrying Fraulein Albertina Fosswinkel.'

"You may fancy what I felt when this atrocious proposition was made to me. I said: 'Dearest Herr Professor! You make my very heart bleed. Waltzing is a horrible and improper thing; and Fraulein Albertina Fosswinkel was waltzing upstairs there, in a wedding dress, with a young gentleman who is not familiar to me, so inappropriately that I found myself unable to watch. But still, for all that, I cannot let this exquisite creature go.' The words were scarcely out of my mouth, when that awful, abominable goldsmith gave me a shove, which made me begin immediately to spin round and round, and, as if propelled by some unknown power, I went waltzing up and down Spandauerstrasse, with my arms clasped around – not a lady, but a broom, which scratched my face. Invisible hands were beating my back as I spun around in this devilish dance. Worse, wherever I turned, the place was swarming with Tussmanns waltzing with their arms around brooms. At last I fell down exhausted, and lost my consciousness. When the light shone into my eyes in the morning – oh, Fosswinkel, share my terror! – I found myself sitting up on the horse of the Kurfürst's statue, in front of him, with my head on his cold, iron breast. Luckily the sentry must have been asleep, for I managed to get down without being seen, at the risk of my life, and got away. I ran to Spandauerstrasse; but I got so terribly frightened again that I had to come here to see you."

"Come now, old fellow," Fosswinkel said. "Do you think I'm going to believe all this rubbish? Did anybody ever hear of anything of this sort happening in our good old city of Berlin?"

"Now," said Tussmann, "you can see for yourself what kind of confusion can arise from the fact that you never *read* anything? If you had read "Microchronicon marchicum" by Hafftitii, the rector of both the Berlin's and the Koln on Spree schools, you would have known that much more extraordinary things can happen. In fact, I go so far as to assert, and to feel quite convinced, that this goldsmith is the very Devil, in *propria persona*."

"Pooh, pooh!" said Fosswinkel, "I wish you wouldn't talk such nonsense. Think a little. What happened was you got drunk, and then went and climbed up onto the Kurfürst's statue."

Tussmann's eyes filled with tears; but Fosswinkel grew graver and graver, and at last said:

"The more I think of it, the more I feel convinced that those people you met were old Manasseh, whom I know very well, and the goldsmith Leonhard, who visits Berlin every now and then. True, I may have not read as many books as you; but, for all that, I know well enough that both of these men are good and honest fellows, and have no more to do with dark magic than you or I. I'm astonished that you, with your knowledge of law, are unaware that superstition is illegal, and forbidden under severe penalties; no practitioner of dark magic could get a license from the government to carry it on, under any circumstances. Look here, Tussmann. I hope there is no foundation for the idea which has just now come into my head. No! I can't believe that you've changed your mind about marrying my daughter; that you are making up all sorts of nonsense to confuse me; that you are going to say to me, 'commission councilor: you and I are men of the world, and I can't marry your daughter, because, if I do, the Devil will bolt away with my legs and beat me black and blue!' It would be too bad, Tussmann, if you were to try on a trick of that sort upon me."

Tussmann could not find words to express his indignation at this notion on the part of his old friend. He vowed, over and over again, that he was most devotedly in love with Albertina; that he would die for her without the least hesitation, like a Leander or a Troilus, and that the Devil might beat him black and blue, in his innocence, as a martyr, rather than he should give Albertina up.

As he was making these assertions, they heard a loud knocking at the door, and in came none other than old Manasseh of whom Fosswinkel had been speaking.

As soon as Tussmann saw him he cried out: "Oh, gracious powers of Heaven! This is the old man who made gold pieces out of a radish, and threw them into the goldsmith's face! The dreadful goldsmith will be coming next, I suppose."

He was about to bolt out the door, but

Fosswinkel held him fast, saying: "Wait till we see what happens." And, turning to the old man, he told him what Tussmann had said about the events of the previous night in the wine shop in Alexanderplatz.

Manasseh looked at Tussmann with a malignant grin, and said: "I have no idea what the gentleman means. Last night, I was sitting in a wine shop, taking a glass of wine to refresh myself after a day of hard work, when this gentleman walked in with Leonhard, the goldsmith. The gentleman drank rather more than was good for him: he couldn't stand up straight, and went out to the street staggering."

"Don't you see," Fosswinkel said, "this is what comes of that terrible habit of liquoring up? You'll have to stop it, if you're going to be my son-in-law."

Tussmann sank down into a chair breathless, closed his eyes, and murmured something unintelligible.

"Of course," said Fosswinkel, "this is what you would feel like after a night of drinking and debauchery." And, in spite of Tussmann's protests Fosswinkel wrapped a white handkerchief around his head and sent him home to Spandauerstrasse in a cab.

"And what's *your* news, Manasseh?" the

commission councilor inquired.

Manasseh smiled and suggested that Herr Fosswinkel probably had no idea what kind of a pleasant news he was bringing. In response to the commission councilor's questioning, he revealed that his nephew Benjamin Dümmerl, a most attractive young fellow worth close to a million in wealth, who had received the title of a baron in Vienna on account of his remarkable merits, had recently returned back from Italy. And that this very same nephew had fallen desperately in love with Fraulein Albertina and would like to offer her his hand in marriage.

It should be noted that the young Baron Dümmerl could be often seen in theaters, where he normally sat in a box of the first tier; even more often did he attend concerts of every description. Everyone knew that he was tall, and as thin as a broom handle; that his thick curly hair and sideburns looked particularly unruly; that his dress was always extravagant, even if styled in the very latest English fashion. He could speak several languages, but had quite a distinct accent in all of them. He could also scrape a tune on a violin, compose short verses, tap out music on the piano, and prided himself on being an art connoisseur without any knowledge of art. People knew him as being witty without wit, a thinker without an ability to think – as well as a fellow who was downright stupid, pushy, noisy, and annoying. In short, to use the concise expressions common in high society he strived to belong to, he was an insufferable snob and a bore. When we add to all this that despite his wealth he was greedy and petty, it was obvious that even the lowliest of people would likely prefer to stay away from him.

When Manasseh mentioned his nephew, the thought of the million in wealth that Benjie possessed passed through the commission councilor's mind; but along with that thought came another, which made the idea of the baron as a son in law seem impossible.

"My good Manasseh, isn't it true that your nephew, like yourself, belongs to the old religion, and therefore – "

"Ho!" cried Manasseh, "what does *that* matter? My nephew is in love with your daughter, and wants to make her happy. A drop or two of holy water won't make much difference to him. He'll be the same man still. You just think the matter over, Herr commission councilor; I shall come back in a day or two with my dear baron, and get your answer." With this, Manasseh took his departure.

Fosswinkel began to think over the affair at once, but despite his normal lack of principles, he simply could not bear the idea of Albertina marrying that disgusting Benjamin, and in a sudden attack of rectitude he determined that he would keep his word to Tussmann.

CHAPTER 4

which tells of portraits, green faces, jumping mice, and old curses

Soon after Albertina met Edmund, she came to the conclusion that the large oil portrait of her father hanging in her room was very poorly painted and didn't look like him at all. She pointed out to her father that though it was so many years since the portrait was painted, he was really looking much younger, and better, than the painter had represented him. She particularly disliked the gloomy, sulky expression of the face, the old-fashioned clothes, and a preposterous bunch of flowers which he was holding delicately between his fingers, adorned with heavy diamond rings.

She kept on the subject so long that at last her father agreed that the portrait was horrible, and that he couldn't understand how the painter had managed to turn out such a caricature of his good-looking person. The more he looked at the picture, the more he was convinced that it was a piece of trash. Finally he decided to take it down, and stow it away in the lumber room.

Albertina heartily agreed with this decision, but mentioned that she was so accustomed to see dear papa's picture in her room that she finds it unbearable to look at the bare space on her wall. The only way out of this situation would be to have a new portrait of dear papa commissioned, this time to a talented artist who would be able to capture the likeness to the original. In fact, she could think of no one else but Edmund Lehsen, an upcoming talent who had already painted a number of exquisite and extremely life-like portraits.

"My dear," the commission councilor said. "You don't know what you're asking for. Those young painters tend to be so proud and condescending, and they always ask an unrealistic price for quite an average piece. They won't think of anything but gold Fredericks, they won't even look at silver thalers."

Albertina started assuring her father that Edmund Lehsen painted for the love of art rather than for money, and would be sure to charge very little. And she kept on at her father so assiduously that at last he agreed to go to Edmund Lehsen and see what he would say about a portrait.

It is easy to imagine the delight with which Edmund expressed his readiness to undertake the commission councilor's portrait; and his delight became rapture when he heard that it was Albertina who put the idea into her father's head. He realized, of course, that this plan would give them plenty of opportunities to see each other. Understandably, when the commission councilor asked, rather anxiously, about the price, Edmund assured him that he wouldn't think of asking for money, and that the honor of being admitted, for the sake of art, into the house of the commission councilor, was more of a reward than he could ever hope for.

"Good Heavens! Can I believe my ears?" the commission councilor said. "No money, dearest Herr Lehsen? No gold Fredericks for your trouble? Not even the expense of your paints and canvas?"

Edmund assured him with a smile that all these things were too insignificant to be taken into account.

"But," Fosswinkel said, "I'm not sure you realize that I'm thinking of a life-size portrait all the way down to my knees."

"It doesn't matter in the slightest," the painter assured.

Tears of joy rose into the commission councilor's eyes as he pressed Edmund warmly to his heart. "Oh, heavenly powers! Are there truly such pure human souls left in our wicked world? First cigars, and now this picture. You are a marvelous man – a marvelous young man, I should say. Dear Herr Lehsen, your soul is full of such virtue, such true purity, which so are rare in these times. But let me tell you, though I am a commission councilor, and I dress in French fashions, I am quite of the same way of thinking as yourself. I can appreciate your large mind, and am as unselfish, and as free with my money, as anybody in the land."

Crafty Fraulein Albertina had, of course, known exactly how Edmund would proceed with her father's commission. Her idea worked. Fosswinkel overflowed with praise for the wonderful young fellow, so entirely free from the least trace of greediness. In the end, he even suggested that Albertina knit a coin purse for Edmund, and, if she saw no particular objection, even weave in a lock of her beautiful chestnut hair, for he knew that young men – especially artists – place a special meaning in objects belonging to beautiful girls. He assured Albertina that if she chose to do something like this for Edmund, she had his full permission, and he would explain it to Tussmann himself. Albertina had not the remotest notion what Tussmann might have to say to the matter, but she did not take the trouble to inquire.

Edmund had his painting gear taken to Fosswinkel's house the very same evening, and the next morning he made his appearance for the first sitting.

He begged the commission councilor to think of the very happiest moment of his life. For instance, when his dead wife first said she loved him, or when Albertina was born, or when he unexpectedly saw some dear friend whom he had thought to be lost to him; and to try and look as he had done then.

"Wait a moment, Herr Lehsen," said Fosswinkel; "I know what to do. One day, about three months ago, I got a letter from Hamburg telling me I won a big prize in the lottery. I ran to my daughter with the letter in my hand. That was the happiest moment I ever had in all my life. Let's choose *that* one; and, just to place the whole thing more vividly before your eyes – and mine – I'll go and get the letter, and you can paint me with the letter it in my hand – just as I was when it came."

So Edmund had to paint Fosswinkel with the letter; he was even asked to make the writing in the letter legible and distinct, word for word, as follows: –

"Respected Sir, I have the honor to inform you –" and so forth. Moreover, the envelope had to be portrayed lying on a little table, so that the address on it, displaying all the commission councilor's official titles written out at full length, could be clearly read. Edmund even had to copy the post mark.

Overall, he painted a good-looking, well-mannered, handsomely dressed man, who *did* bear a distant resemblance to the commission councilor, so that nobody who read what was on the envelope could make any mistake as to whom the portrait showed.

Herr Fosswinkel was delighted.

"There," he said, "there you see what an artist who knows his business can make of a more or less well-looking fellow, though he *may* be getting a little on in years! I begin to understand now a thing that our professor in the humanity class used to say, that a proper portrait has to be an authentic historical painting. Whenever I look at that one, I remember the joyous moment when the news came of my prize in the lottery, and I understand the meaning of that smile on my face – the reflection of the happiness I felt within me then."

Before Albertina could even hint at the next step in her plans, her father preempted her by begging Edmund to paint her portrait as well.

Edmund began this work at once. But he did not find it so easy to satisfy himself with her portrait as with her father's. He put in a most careful outline, and then erased it again; outlined once more – carefully – began to lay on some color, and then threw the whole thing aside; commenced again; altered the pose. There was always either too much light in the room, or not enough. The commission councilor, who had always been present at those sittings at first, got tired eventually, and stopped coming.

Now Edmund was in the house both in the morning and at night, and if the picture did not make much progress, the mutual affection between him and Albertina grew stronger every day.

I have no doubt, dear reader, that you can relate to a situation when a person in love feels the need to convey their feelings by holding the hand of the beloved object, pressing it, and kissing it. At such moment, as if driven by electrical force, lips find each other; and the electrical current resolves in an overwhelming stream of passionate kisses. When this happened, Edmund not only had to interrupt his work, but sometimes even to step away from his easel.

This is how it happened that one morning he found himself standing with Albertina beside the window, covered by white curtains, and (on the principle we have been explaining), to reinforce whatever he was saying to her at the moment, he had no choice but to hold her in his arms and kiss her.

At this particular moment, Herr Tussmann, the chancery clerk, was passing Fosswinkel's house, his pockets filled with the "Treatise on Diplomatic Acumen" and a number of equally entertaining and useful old books. Although he was in a hurry, because the clock was just on the very stroke of the hour at which he always entered his office, he paused for a moment and lifted his head to cast a sentimental glance up at the window of his bride.

As if in a daze, he saw Albertina with Edmund; and, although he could not make out anything distinctly, his heart skipped a beat. He felt a surge of panic that prompted him to do something he would never consider before: to enter the house unannounced and go upstairs straight to Albertina's rooms, at this totally unprecedented hour of the day.

As he entered, Albertina was saying, quite distinctly:

"Oh, yes, Edmund! I will always – always love you!" And Edmund pressed her to his heart, followed by an explosion of aforementioned electrical charges.

Inadvertently, Tussmann took a step forward and stopped, dumb and speechless, like a man in a cataleptic fit. In the height of their bliss the two lovers had not heard the sound of the door, or the heavy tread of Tussmann's peculiar boots. Not until he squeaked out, in his high falsetto:

"What is the meaning of this, Fraulein Albertina Fosswinkel?"

Edmund and Albertina fled apart – he to

his easel, she to the chair where she was supposed to be sitting for her portrait.

Tussmann took a few breaths, steadying his voice. "Fraulein Albertina Fosswinkel, what are you doing? What kind of a conduct is this? First, you go out and waltz with this young gentleman (I haven't had the honor of his acquaintance), in the town hall at midnight, in a way that has made me, your husband to be, almost lose my mind; and now, here, in broad daylight, behind those curtains – Oh! Good gracious! – is this a way for an engaged young lady to behave?"

"Who's an engaged young lady?" Albertina demanded. "Whom are you talking about, Herr Tussmann? Tell me, if you would be so kind."

"Oh, thou, my Creator," wailed Tussmann. "How can you possibly ask such a thing? Who else may I be talking about if not you? Are you not my future bride, whom I have so long adored in secret? Did not your dear papa ever so long ago, promise me your beautiful, white, kissable little hand in marriage?"

"Herr Tussmann," said Albertina; "either you have been to a wine shop, early as it is in the day – (my father says you go to them a great deal more than you ought), – or you've gone out of your mind in some extraordinary way. My father could never have possibly had the slightest idea of *you* marrying *me*."

"Dearest Fraulein Albertina," Tussmann said. "Consider this for a moment. You have known me for many long years. Have I not always been a man of the strictest moderation and temperance? Can you suppose that I have taken to drinking and improper conduct all in one day? Dearest Fraulein Albertina, I shall be only too happy to close my eyes to what I have seen going on here; not a syllable concerning it shall ever pass my lips – we'll forget and forgive. But remember, adored one, that you promised to marry me out of the tower window of the town hall at the night of the autumnal equinox; and, although you were waltzing in such a style with this young gentleman (whose acquaintance, as I said, I have not had the honor of), still I –"

"Don't you see?" interrupted Albertina. "You're talking all sorts of incoherent nonsense, like some lunatic out of an asylum? Please go away. I feel quite unwell; do go away, for goodness' sake."

Tears filled Tussmann's eyes.

"Oh, heavens!" he cried. "Treatment like this from my beloved Fraulein Albertina! No; I shall not go. I shall remain here till you have arrived at a truer opinion concerning my unworthy person, dearest Fraulein Albertina."

"Go away!" Albertina ran into a corner of the room, and covered her face with a handkerchief.

"No, dearest Fraulein Albertina," answered Tussmann; "I shall not go until, in compliance with the sapient advice of Thomasius, I endeavor to – " He started following her into the corner.

While this was going on, Edmund had been dabbing angrily at the background of his picture. But at this point he could contain himself no longer.

"You scoundrel!" he cried, and flew at Tussmann, making four dashes over his face with the brush, full of a greyish green tint, which he had been working at his background with. Then he grasped the chancery clerk, opened the door, and sent him out with a kick so forcible that the unfortunate man went flying down stairs like an arrow out of a bow.

Fosswinkel, who was just coming up, started back in much alarm as his school friend came bumping down into his arms.

"What in the name of all that's –" he cried. "What's going on? What ails your face?"

Tussmann, almost out of his mind,

related all that had happened, in broken phrases; how Albertina had behaved to him – how Edmund had treated him. The commission councilor, brimming with fury, took Tussmann by the hand and led him back into the room.

"What's all this?" he said to Albertina. "Is this the way you treat your husband to be?"

"My husband to be?" echoed Albertina, wide-eyed.

"Most undoubtedly," the commission councilor answered. "I don't know why you should pretend to be in a state of mind about a matter which has been understood and arranged for such a long time. My dear old friend Tussmann is your fiancé, and the wedding will take place in a week or two."

"*Never!*" said Albertina. "I will never marry him. Good heavens, how could anybody even think of marrying *that* old creature; I couldn't bear the sight of him."

"I don't know about 'bearing' him, or whether he's an 'old creature' or not," said her father. "What you have got to do is to marry him. Certainly my friend Tussmann is not one of your giddy young fools. Like myself, he has reached those years of discretion when a man is, very properly, considered to be at his best; he is a fine, upright, straightforward, honorable fellow, most profoundly learned, perfectly eligible in every way, and my old schoolfellow."

"No!" Tears rolled from Albertina's eyes. "I can't endure him. I hate him! I abhor him! Oh, Edmund!"

She sank into Edmund's arms; and he pressed her to his heart with the warmest affection.

The commission councilor, utterly amazed, opened his eyes as wide as if he were seeing ghosts, and then cried: "What's all this? What do I see?"

"Ah, yes! Yes, indeed!" Tussmann said, in a lamentable tone. "It appears, unfortunately, to be the fact that Fraulein Albertina doesn't care to have anything to do with me, and seems to cherish a remarkable partiality for this young gentleman – this painter (whose acquaintance I have not had the honor of, by the way) – inasmuch as she kisses him without the slightest hesitation or shyness, though she will scarcely give the wretched *me* her hand. And yet I hope to place the ring on her lovely finger very shortly indeed."

"Come away from one another, you two," the commission councilor cried out, and forced Albertina out of Edmund's arms. But Edmund shouted that he would never give her up, if it cost him his life.

"Indeed, sir!" said the commission councilor, with scathing irony. "Nice business, upon my word! A fine little love-affair going on behind my back here! Excessively pretty! Very nice indeed, my young Herr Lehsen! This is the meaning of your liberality, as well as, I suppose, your cigars and your pictures. He snakes his way into my house – and into my daughter's confidence. Whatever gave you the preposterous idea that I would ever agree to push my daughter into the arms of a miserable, poor, talentless beggar?"

Beyond himself with anger, Edmund raised his mahlstick, when Leonhard burst in through the door –

"Stop, Edmund! Don't be in such a hurry. Fosswinkel is an idiot, but he'll come around soon."

The commission councilor ran into a corner, frightened by the unexpected arrival of Leonhard; and, from that corner, he cried: "I really do not know, Herr Leonhard, how dare you – "

Tussmann had hidden himself behind the sofa as soon as he saw Leonhard come in. Crouching down there, he wailed: "Gracious powers! Be careful, commission councilor! Hold your tongue; don't say a word, dearest schoolfellow. Good God! This is Herr Professor I spoke to you about, the merciless dance master of Spandauer-strasse."

"Come out, Tussmann," said the goldsmith, laughing; "Don't be frightened, nothing's going to happen to you. You've been punished enough already for that foolish idea of wanting to marry, for your face is going to remain green for the rest of your life."

"Oh Lord!" wailed the chancery clerk. "My face, green for ever and ever! What will people say? What will His Excellency, the minister, say? His Excellency will think I have had my face painted green out of some foolish vanity! I am all finished, I shall be suspended from my official functions. The government will never allow such a thing as a chancery clerk with a green face. Oh, what's to become of me?"

"Come, come, Tussmann!" the goldsmith said; "don't make such a fuss. I have no doubt there's hope for you yet, if you pull yourself together, and get rid of this idiotic notion of marrying Fraulein Fosswinkel."

In answer to this, Tussmann and Fosswinkel cried out together, in what is termed "*ensemble*" on the lyric stage:

"I can't."

"He won't."

The goldsmith fixed his piercing eyes on both of them; but at that moment the door opened, and in came Manasseh with his nephew, Baron Benjamin Dümmerl from Vienna. Benjie went straight up to Albertina – who had never seen him in her life before – and took her hand, speaking in his creaky voice –

"I have come here in person, dear Fraulein Fosswinkel, to lay myself at your feet. Of course you know this is a mere *façon de parler*. Baron Dümmerl doesn't really lay himself at anybody's feet, not even at the Emperor's. What I mean is – let me have a kiss."

So saying, he drew Albertina into his arms, and bent down towards her.

But, at that moment, Benjie's rather sizeable nose suddenly shot forward past Albertina's face and struck the wall behind her with a loud bang. Benjie drew back and his nose at once shortened in to its ordinary length. Every time he leaned toward Albertina, his nose elongated again, so that as Benje kept trying to kiss her, it kept on shooting in and out like a trombone.

"You cursed necromancer!" Manasseh roared. He took out a cord with a knot and tossed it to the commission councilor, crying: "Throw it around the damned glodsmith's neck! Never mind about ceremony. As soon as you do, you and I would have no trouble dragging the devil out of here."

The commission councilor caught the noose, but instead of throwing it around the goldsmith's neck, he threw it over Manasseh's; and immediately he and the old man jumped up to the ceiling. They went on, jumping up and down, while Benjie carried on his nose-concerto, and Tussmann laughed maniacally, until the commission councilor finally collapsed in an armchair.

"Now's the time! Now's the time!" Manasseh cried. He slapped his pocket, and out sprung an enormous, horrible-looking mouse, which jumped right at the goldsmith. But the goldsmith pierced it with a sharp golden needle. It screamed and disappeared.

Then Manasseh clenched his fists and rushed at the commission councilor, shouting:

"Ha! Melchior Fosswinkel! You have conspired against me. You are in league with this accursed sorcerer. Cursed, cursed you will be. Your entire line will wither away. Grass will grow on your doorstep, and all that you set your hand to shall crumble to dust. And Dahles shall take up his dwelling in your house, and consume all your wealth.

You will beg for bread, in rags, before the doors of the despised people of God; and they shall drive you away like a mangy cur, and you will be cast to the earth like a rotten branch. And instead of the sound of the harp, moths shall be your fellows, and dogs shall make a bed on the tomb of your mother! Curses! – curses! – curses upon you, commission councilor Melchior Fosswinkel!"

With that, Manasseh seized his nephew and stormed out of the house.

Albertina, in her terror, had taken refuge with Edmund, hiding her face on his breast; and he held her closely, though he had difficulty controlling his own emotion.

The goldsmith stepped up to the couple and said, with a smile:

"Don't you be put out in the slightest by all this business: everything will be all right. I give you my word for it. But, just now, you must bid each other good bye, before Tussmann and Fosswinkel come back to their senses."

And he and Edmund left Fosswinkel's house.

CHAPTER 5

where we learn about Dahles, as well as how the goldsmith saved the chancery clerk Tussmann from a miserable death and comforted the despairing commission councilor

Fosswinkel felt utterly shaken. He was even more troubled by Manasseh's curse than by the wild piece of trickery the goldsmith performed. And indeed it was a terrible curse, for it set Dahles on to him.

Dear reader, I don't know if you are aware what Dahles is.

One of the Talmudists says that one day, a poor man's wife coming into her house, found an emaciated naked stranger there, who begged her to give him the shelter of her roof, and food and drink. She went to her husband, and told him: "A naked, starving man has come in, asking for food and shelter. How are we to help him, when we barely have enough for ourselves?" The husband said: "I will go to this stranger, and see how I can get him out of the house."

"Can't you see that we are so poor we can't help you?" he said to the stranger. "Begone! Go to a rich man's house, where the cattle are fat, and the guests are bidden to the feast!"

"How can you drive me away?" said the stranger. "You see that I am bare and naked: how can I go to a rich man's house? Give me some clothes, and I will leave." "Better," thought the master of the house, "better it is for me to spend all I possess in getting rid of him, than having him stay and consume whatever I earn in the time to come." So he killed his last calf, on which he and his wife had thought to live for many days, sold the meat, and used the money to buy clothes for the stranger. But when he took the clothes to his guest, he found that the stranger, who had before been lean and short of stature, had become tall and stout, so that the clothing was too short and too narrow to fit him anymore. The poor man was horrified, but the stranger said: "Give up the foolish idea of getting me out of thy house. Know that I am Dahles!" The poor man wrung his hands in despair and cried: "God of my fathers! You have punished me beyond measure, for ever and ever! For if this is truly Dahles, he will never leave us, but will consume everything we have, and always grow bigger and stronger. For Dahles is Poverty; which, once it takes up its abode in a house, never departs from it, but ever increases more and more."

If the commission councilor was terrified that Manasseh, by his curse, had brought poverty into his house, he was also frightened of Leonhard, who not only appeared to command extraordinary magical powers, but also was an awe-inspiring person overall. The commission councilor could do nothing about either of these men, so he directed his entire anger at Edmund Lehsen, whom he blamed for bringing about all these troubles. In addition to his woes, Albertina declared that she loved Edmund more than words could express, and would never marry either that insufferable and unendurable old pedant Tussmann, or the not-to-be-heard-of beast Baron Benjamin. As a result, the commission councilor felt so enraged that he wished Edmund to go "where the pepper grows." But since this wish couldn't possibly be granted, as only the late French government did actually have the power to send objectionable persons to the place "where the pepper grows", he had to be content with writing Edmund a nice little note, into which he poured all the gall and venom he had accumulated, and which ended with a request that Edmund never as much as think of crossing the commission councilor's threshold again.

Of course we all know the state of inconsolable despair in which Leonhard found Edmund, when he went to see the young man at the fall of the twilight.

"What have *I* to thank you for?" Edmund said as soon as he saw the goldsmith. "Of what service have your protection and all your efforts been to *me*? Your attempts to remove a rival out of my way – what has been the result of them? Those damnable conjuring tricks of yours – all that *they* have done has been to send everybody into a state of frenzy, where nobody knows what to think anymore! Even my beloved Albertina is afraid now, not to mention that my way to her is irrevocably blocked. The only thing left for me to do is to get away from here. I will leave for Rome at once, and, I can assure you, I mean to do it, too."

"Perfect," the goldsmith said. "This is exactly what I want you to do. Be good enough to remember what I said to you when you first told me you were in love with Albertina. I said my idea was that a young artist has a right to be in love, but that he should not go and marry at once, before he had a chance to learn more about art. When I said that to you, I brought to your mind, half in jest, the case of Sternbald; but now I tell you seriously that, if you really wish to become a great painter, you must put all ideas of marrying out of your head. Go your way, free and unattached, into the motherland of art; study as hard as you can; and then, and only then can you make full use of your talent and potential."

"Good gracious!" Edmund cried, "what an idiot I've been to reveal my love to you. I see, now, that it was you – you, on whom I relied for advice and help – who have been purposely throwing obstacles into my way, playing with my heart desires, out of nastiness and unkindness."

"My good young sir," the goldsmith said. "I would be immensely grateful to you if you dampen your passion. You would be good to remember that you do have a thing or two to learn before you can even guess my intentions. But for the sake of your crazy love, I will hold no grudge against you this time."

"As for the art," Edmund went on, "I really can't see how being engaged to Albertina could prevent me from going to Rome. In fact, I had an idea to spend a whole year in Italy – but only after I am assured that Albertina will be mine. Then, enriched by my knowledge of the sacred skills of the art, I would be able to return and embrace my bride."

"Really, Edmund?" the goldsmith said. "Was this really what you were planning to do?"

"Yes," Edmund answered. "Deeply as I love Albertina, my heart longs for the great motherland of my beloved art."

"Will you give me your solemn word," the goldsmith said, "that once you are sure that Albertina will be yours, you will be off at once to Italy?"

"I will," Edmund said. "I've made my

decision and will not change it if that which I dare not even hope for can truly happen."

"Well, Edmund," the goldsmith said, "in this case, do not despair. Your firm resolve has gained you your sweetheart. I give you my word of honor that in no more than a few days Albertina will be your bride. I hope you know by now that you need not doubt my power to keep my word."

Joy lit up Edmund's eyes; and the mysterious goldsmith went away quickly, leaving him to all the sweet hopes and dreams awakened in his heart.

In a distant corner of the Thiergarten the chancery clerk Herr Tussmann lay under a tall tree – in the words of Celia from "As You Like It", "like a dropped acorn or a wounded knight", passionately confessing his misfortunes to the ever-shifting autumn breeze.

"Oh, God," he lamented. "What a pitiable, ill-fated chancery clerk I am. What did I ever do to deserve all this misery? Did not Herr Thomasius say that the estate of matrimony should in no way hinder the acquisition of wisdom? And yet, although I have only been *thinking* of entering into that estate, I've nearly lost my mind. Why would my dear Fraulein Fosswinkel despise me so passionately? In all modesty, I must still point out that I possess many virtues one would find desirable in a husband. I am not a politician, or an expert in the laws, who (according to Cleobolus) ought to give his wife a licking if she misbehaves herself? Why would my beautiful Albertina resist this marriage so much? Oh, dear God, what an ill-fated chancery clerk I am. How could a peaceful man like me get mixed up with horrible wizards and raging painters, who took my face for a stretched canvas, and painted a Salvator Rosa picture on it without my consent? What could possibly be worse? I've put all my trust in my friend, Herr Seccius, whose knowledge of chemistry is so extensive and so profound, and who can help people out of every difficulty. But all in vain. The more I rub my face with the ointment he's given me, the greener it gets. Worse, with each application the green color takes on the most extraordinary variety of different tints and shades. My face has gone through the colors of spring, summer, and autumn. This greenness will surely become my destruction, and if I don't manage to attain the whiteness of winter (the proper color for me), I shall most certainly despair and plunge myself into the disgusting frog pond here, to die a green death!"

Tussmann had every right to complain so

bitterly. His green face indeed made his life miserable, for it wasn't like any ordinary oil color, but some cleverly compounded tincture that penetrated into his skin and could not to be obliterated by any human means. In the daytime the poor chancery clerk had to go out with his hat pushed all the way forward over his eyes, covering the rest of his face with his handkerchief. Even at night he could only rush through the more deserted streets at a gallop, to avoid the mockery of the street boys, or worse, coming across somebody from his office, where he had reported himself sick.

We often become more acutely aware of our troubles in the silent hours of the night, rather than during the daylight. This is why, as the sky became darker, as the shadows of the trees fell longer, as the autumn wind sighed louder and louder in the branches, Tussmann had sunk deeper and deeper into his despair.

The idea of jumping into the frog pond, and thus putting an end to his miserable life, had formed so clearly in his head that he had taken it for a stroke of fate he couldn't possibly disobey.

"Yes," he exclaimed, getting up from the grass, where he had been lying. "Yes! It's all over for you, chancery clerk. Despair and die, my good Tussmann. Thomasius can't help you. On, to a green death! Farewell, my cruel Fraulein Albertina Fosswinkel. You would never again see your fiancé, whom you despised so cruelly. Here I go, into the frog-pond!"

Like a mad creature he rushed to the nearby pond, that in the gathering dusk looked like a smooth, wide road, with trees around it), and stopped on the very edge of the water. Doubtless, the notion of the nearness of death affected his mind; for he sang, in a high-pitched, penetrating voice, that Scotch song, which has the refrain –

"Green grow the rashes, oh!
Green grow the rashes!"

And he tossed the "Diplomatic Acumen", and the "Handbook for Court and City", and also "Hufeland, on the Art of Prolonging Life", into the water, and was about to jump in after them, when a pair of powerful arms seized him from behind.

He heard the familiar voice of the evil sorcerer, the goldsmith Leonhard:

"Tussmann, what are you doing? Do me a favor, don't make an ass of yourself; don't go playing idiotic tricks of this sort."

Tussmann tried with all his might to get

out of the goldsmith's grasp as he muttered:

"Herr Professor! I am in a state of desperation, and all ordinary considerations are in abeyance. Herr Professor, I sincerely trust you will not take it ill if a despairing chancery clerk, who is, under ordinary circumstances, well versed in the conventions of the official etiquette – I say, I hope you won't take it ill, Herr Professor, if I assert, openly and unceremoniously, that (under all the circumstances of the case) I wish to heaven that you, and all your magic tricks, as well as your unendurable familiarity, your 'Tussmann! Tussmann!' never giving me my official title! – would go to the Devil!"

The goldsmith let him go, and he tumbled down, exhausted, into the long, wet grass.

Believing himself to be in the pond, he cried out, "Oh, cold death! Oh, green rashes! Oh, meadows! I bid ye farewell. I leave you my kindest wishes, dearest Fraulein Albertina Fosswinkel. Commission councilor, good bye! The unfortunate groom is lying amongst the frogs that praise God in the summer time."

"Tussmann," said the goldsmith, "don't you see that you're out of your mind? You want to send me to the Devil? What if I *am* the Devil, and will wring your neck here on this spot, where you think you're lying in the water?"

Tussmann sighed, groaned, and shuddered.

"But I mean you no harm, Tussmann," the goldsmith said. "I blame your desperate condition for this outburst. Get up, and come along with me." And he helped the chancery clerk up to his feet.

Exhausted, Tussmann continued to mutter:

"I am completely in your power, most honored Herr Professor. Do what you will with my miserable body; but I most humbly beg you to spare my immortal soul."

"Do not talk nonsense, just hurry up." The goldsmith took Tussmann by the arm and led him away. But when they came to the crossroads with the walkway that leads to the Zelten, he stopped and said:

"Wait a moment, Tussmann. You're wet through, and you look like garbage. Let me at least wipe your face."

He took a dazzling white handkerchief out of his pocket, and wiped Tussmann's face with it.

When they reached the brightly lit vicinity of the Weberschen Zelt, Tussmann cried out in alarm –

"For God's sake, Herr Professor, where

are you taking me? Not into town? Not to my own lodgings? Not (oh, heavens!) into society, among my fellow-men? Good heavens, I can't be seen like this... There will be trouble... A scandal!"

"Tussmann," said the goldsmith, "I can't understand why you have to be so shy. Don't be a coward. What you need is a glass of strong wine. I should say a tumbler of hot punch, before you catch cold and come down with a fever. Follow me."

Tussmann kept on lamenting about his greenness, and his Salvator Rosa face; but the goldsmith paid no attention, dragging him along at a fast walk.

When they entered a brightly lit restaurant, Tussmann hid his face in his handkerchief, as several people were still sitting around a long table finishing their dinner.

"What's the matter with you, Tussmann?" the goldsmith whispered into the chancery clerk's ear. "Why do you keep hiding your honest face, eh?"

"Oh, dearest Herr Professor, you know all about my awful face," Tussmann moaned. "You know how that terrible young painter got angry with me and daubed it all over with green paint?"

"Nonsense," said the goldsmith, taking

the chancery clerk by the shoulders and placing him right in front of the big mirror at the end of the room, while he picked up a lit candle from the table to make it brighter.

Tussmann forced himself to look, and gasped.

Not only was his face fully devoid of any green tint, but he had a better complexion than he ever had had in his life, and was looking several years younger.

He couldn't help but jump up and down in delight as he exclaimed: "Oh, Heavens! What do I see? Can this be true? Most honored Herr Professor, I have no doubt that it is to you that I am indebted for this great happiness! – to you alone! Ah! Now I have no doubt that Fraulein Albertina Fosswinkel – for whose dear sake I so very nearly jumped into the frog pond – would have no reservations in accepting me. Really, dearest Professor, you have rescued me from the very profoundest depths of misery. It was your handkerchief, wasn't it, that wiped the ugly color off my face? You really are my benefactor, are you not?"

"I won't deny, Tussmann," the goldsmith answered, "that I did wipe the green color off your face; I hope you take it as evidence that I am not your enemy, as you have probably supposed me to be. What I can't bear is your ridiculous talk – which you have allowed the commission councilor to put in your head – that you are still capable of marrying a beautiful and cheerful young girl. Even now – though you have scarcely cleared yourself of the last trick which has been played on you – you spared no time in starting to talk about this marriage again. I am warning you, I can do so much worse to you and use an enchantment so horrible that it would drive this crazy idea completely out of your head. However, I don't want to do anything like this. Instead, I suggest you to calm down and hold off until next Sunday at noon, when you will learn the rest. But be warned: if you dare to go and see Albertina before that time, I will make you dance in front of her until you fall in exhaustion. Then I will transform you into the very greenest of frogs, and throw you into the pond in the Thiergarten, or into the River Spree, where you'll go on croaking till the end of your days. Good-bye. I have something to do in town. You won't be able to follow me, or keep up with me. Good-bye!"

The goldsmith was right in saying that it would not be possible for Tussmann, or anybody else, to keep up with him, for as he stepped through the door he immediately vanished out of sight, as if he was wearing

Schlemihl's seven-mile boots.

The next minute after he had disappeared from Tussmann's view, he popped out of thin air in front of the commission councilor, and bade him good evening in a rough tone.

The commission councilor was very frightened, but he pulled himself together, and asked the goldsmith what he meant by calling this late the night, adding that he wished he would take his leave immediately, and not bother him any more with any of those devilish tricks, which, as he presumed, he was about to perform.

"Ah," said the goldsmith very calmly, "so this is what commission councilors are like these days. Just when you come to them wishing to do them a service, just as you expect them to throw themselves into your arms – they try to kick out of the door. My good Herr Commission Councilor, you are a very unfortunate man, worthy of my pity and compassion. I have come here – I have *hurried* here – at this late hour of the night, to advise you how to avert the deadly blow about to strike you, before it's too late, and you – "

"Oh, God," the commission councilor wailed, beside himself with fear. "You must be talking about another bankruptcy in Hamburg, Bremen, or London, one that is going to ruin me completely. Oh, I'm a miserable commission councilor!"

"No," the goldsmith said. "I am speaking about a different thing altogether. You say that you won't allow young Edmund Lehsen to marry Albertina, do you not?"

"Is this some sort of a sick joke?" the commission councilor demanded. "To even think that I would allow my only daughter to marry such a talentless dauber."

"Well," said the goldsmith, "he has painted magnificent portraits of you and Albertina."

"What a curious thought," said Fosswinkel, "to expect me to sell my daughter for a couple of cheap pictures. I've sent the trash back to him."

"If you don't let Edmund have your daughter," the goldsmith continued, "he will take his revenge on you."

"I would love to know," said Fosswinkel, "what kind of revenge can this penniless beggar, who dribbles paints on canvas and hasn't a farthing to his name, possibly take upon the commission councilor Melchior Fosswinkel?"

"I'll tell you that in a moment," said the Goldsmith. "Edmund is going to alter your portrait in a way which you thoroughly deserve. He will turn your kind smiling face into a sour, grumpy one, emphasizing the wrinkles on your forehead and cheeks, you bleary eyes, and downturned lips. He will also reveal the grey hair which you are hiding with so much effort under a layer of powder. Instead of the joyous news about the lottery prize, he will paint you holding the letter you received yesterday, informing you about the bankruptcy of Campbell and Co. in London, addressed on the envelope to the 'The failed Herr Municipal Councilor' – for it is known to him that about six month ago you tried and failed to attain this title. He will paint you with torn waistcoat pockets, spilling out ducats, thalers, and treasury bills, to symbolize the losses you have had, and this portrait will be displayed in the front window of the art shop next door to the bank in Yaggerstrasse."

"The demon, the blackguard," the commission councilor exclaimed. "I won't allow him to do that. I'll call the police, I'll sue him in court."

"Perhaps," the goldsmith said calmly. "But as soon as at least fifty people have seen this picture, which would take no more than a quarter of an hour of window display, they will spread the news all over town, with all kinds of additions and exaggeration. Everything in the least degree ridiculous which has ever been said about you, or is being said now, will be brought up again, dressed in fresh and vibrant colors. Everyone you meet will laugh in your face, and, what is the worst of all, everybody will talk about your losses in the Campbell bankruptcy, so your credit will be gone."

"Oh, Lord," said Fosswinkel, "but he must let me have the picture back, the scoundrel? Aye; that he must, the first thing in the morning."

"And if he were to agree to do so," the goldsmith said, "of which I have great doubts, how could it possibly help you? He can make a copper etching of you, the way I have just described you, and print hundreds of copies, so that he can color them *con amore*, and send them all over the world – to Hamburg, Bremen, Lübeck, even to London – "

"Enough, enough," Fosswinkel cried; "go, as fast as you can, to this terrible fellow; offer him fifty, no, a hundred thalers for his promise to leave my portrait alone."

"Ha! ha! ha!" laughed the goldsmith; "you forget that Lehsen doesn't care a bit about money. His parents are well off. Besides, his grand-aunt, Fraulein Lehsen, who lives in Breitstrasse, has named him the sole heir of her estate – no less than eighty thousand thalers."

"What?" The commission councilor paled with amazement. "Eighty thousand... Listen, Herr Leonhard, it seems to me that my beloved daughter is crazy about young Lehsen... As a kind-hearted fellow and a loving father, I can't possibly stand in the way of my daughter's happiness... When she sets her heart on something, I can't refuse her. Besides, I like the fellow. He's a superb painter, and you know I have a soft spot for art. The good man Lehsen has so many admirable qualities... Eighty thousand... You know what, Herr Leonhard, just out of my pure good-heartedness, I shall let this nice young fellow have my daughter."

"Hm!" said the goldsmith. "In this case, I must also tell you something curious. I've been walking at the Thiergarten just before I came here, and I found your old friend and schoolfellow, Tussmann, getting ready to jump into a pond because Albertina has rejected him. I had the greatest difficulty in preventing him from doing it; and it was only by telling him that you would be quite certain to keep your word, and make her marry him, that I did succeed. Now, if this is not so, if she doesn't marry him, and if you give her to young Lehsen, there is no doubt that the chancery clerk is going to carry out his idea of drowning himself in that pond. Think what kind of rumors could arise from the suicide of such a respectable man. Everybody will consider that you, and none other, are responsible for his death. You will be looked on with horror and contempt. Nobody will ask you to dinner, and if you go to a tavern to see what's in the papers, you will be shown to the door, or thrown down the stairs. Worse, your friend Tussmann is so highly valued in his profession, and all his superiors have a very high opinion of him; the Government departments think him a most valuable official. If you become known as the man responsible for his death, you will never find a single member of the Privy Legation, or of the Upper Chamber of Finance who would be willing to do business with you. None of the offices which your business affairs require you to be *en rapport* with will have a word to say to you. Your title of commission councilor will be taken from you, blow will follow upon blow, your credit will be gone, your income will melt away, things will go from bad to worse, till at last, in poverty, misery and contempt, you will – "

"For God's sake stop!" cried the commission councilor. "You are tormenting me. Who would have thought that Tussmann, in his advanced years, would become such a love-sick baboon? But you are quite right; whatever happens, I must keep my word to him, or I'm a ruined man. Yes, it is decided. Tussmann will marry Albertina."

"You're forgetting all about Baron Dümmerl," said the goldsmith, "and Manasseh's terrible curse. If you reject Baron Benjie, the old man will become a dangerous enemy. He will oppose you at every turn; he will spare no means to harm your credit; he will use every possible opportunity to block every one of your undertakings. He will never rest until he brings you to shame and disgrace, till Dahles, which he has called upon you with his curse, has actually taken up its abode in your house. In short, whatever you decided to do with Albertina, whoever you give her hand in marriage to, you get into trouble. This is why, at the beginning of our conversation, I've called you a very unfortunate man, worthy of my pity and compassion."

Fosswinkel rushed up and down the room like a lunatic, crying over and over again, "It's all over with me. I am a miserable man, a ruined commission councilor. O Lord, if only I could find a way to her the girl off my hands. The Devil take the whole lot of them, Lehsen, and Benjie, and my old friend Tussmann too."

"Come, come," said the goldsmith. "There's still a way to get you out of this mess."

"What way?" Fosswinkel stopped, staring at Leonhard. "What way? I will do anything!"

"Have you ever seen the play 'The Merchant of Venice'?" Leonhard said.

"Is this the play," answered Fosswinkel, "where Devrient plays a bloodthirsty man by the name of Shylock, who wants a pound of a merchant's flesh? Of course I've seen it, but what does it have to do with my situation?"

"You may remember in 'The Merchant of Venice'," the goldsmith said, "a wealthy young lady by the name of Portia, whose father's will declared that she will become the wife of anyone who wins a special kind of a lottery. Each of her suitors must choose one of the three chests, and open it. The one who finds Portia's portrait in the chest wins her hand. I suggest that you, commission councilor, do the same. Tell the three suitors that you favor them all equally, and thus will rely on chance to decide between them. Set up three chests for them to choose from, and let the one who finds her portrait in his chest be her husband."

"What an extraordinary idea," said the commission councilor. "Do you believe, dear Herr Leonhard, that this would truly help my situation? What if, after the matter is decided by chance, I am faced with the rage and hatred of the unsuccessful two?"

"Wait," the goldsmith said. "This is the most important part. I give you my solemn promise that I will provide and arrange the chests in the way that the lottery will turn out happily and satisfactorily for all parties. The two who do not choose Albertina will find not merely a scornful dismissal in their chests, like the Princes of Morocco and Aragon, but will acquire something that will so greatly please and delight them that they will think no more of marrying Albertina, but will look upon you as the perpetrator of ultimate happiness for them."

"Oh, if only it were possible!" the commission councilor exclaimed.

"Not only is it possible," the goldsmith said, "but it will happen exactly as I said, you have my word."

The commission councilor made no further objections, and they decided that the ceremony of choosing the bride should take place next Sunday at noon. Leonhard promised to provide the three chests, all ready.

CHAPTER 6

where the bride is chosen and this tale is concluded

As may be imagined, Albertina fell into despair when her father told her about the wretched lottery, in which her hand was to be the prize. No amount of begging and tears could convince him to abandon the idea. To make it worse, Lehsen seemed indifferent and passive, not the way a man in love was expected to act. He had made no attempt to see her privately, or even to send her a message.

On the night before the fateful Sunday Albertina was sitting alone in her room. As the twilight was deepening into the night, she felt more and more absorbed in her misery. She even wondered whether it would be better to run away from home, rather than being married off to the pedantic old Tussmann, or worse, to the insufferable Baron Benjamin. But just then she remembered the mysterious goldsmith, and the magical way in which he had prevented the Baron from touching her. She felt quite sure that the goldsmith was on Edmund's side; and this certainty made her hopeful that this was the man she could rely on in this critical situation. She wished she could talk to him; and, deep inside, she felt quite sure that if he were to appear to her magically right now, she wouldn't be frightened at all.

Indeed, she didn't feel in the least frightened when she realized that the object in the depths of the room that she had been taking for the stove was really Leonhard the goldsmith, who came up to her and said, in a deep, gentle voice:

"My dear child, lay aside all grief and anxiety. I want you to know that Edmund Lehsen, whom you love – or at least you believe you love – is a *protégé* of mine, and I am helping him with all the power at my command. Let me further tell you that it was I who put the lottery idea into your father's head; that I am going to provide and prepare the chests, and, of course, it must be clear to you now that no one but Edmund will find your portrait."

Albertina felt beside herself with joy, while the goldsmith continued:

"I could have achieved your betrothal to Edmund in different ways; but I wanted to make sure the two other rivals for your hand, Tussmann and the Baron, are fully satisfied. After tomorrow, you and your father can rest assured you will have nothing to fear from either of them."

Albertina poured out her warmest thanks. She felt ready to fall at the goldsmith's feet as she pressed his hand to her heart and declared that, despite all his magic tricks, she wasn't in the least afraid of him; and in the end she asked him, rather naively, if he could tell her all about himself, and who he really was.

"My dear child," the goldsmith said with a smile. "It's not as easy as you think to tell you exactly who I am. Like many others, I know much better what I am believed to be, rather than what I really and truly am myself. But I may tell you, my dear, that many think I am none other than Leonhard Turnhäuser the Goldsmith – a famous character at the court of the Kurfürst

Johann Georg, who in the year 1580 disappeared, none knew how or where, when envy and calumny tried to ruin him. You understand, of course, that people who believe that I am this Turnhäuser, a spectral being, are romantics and dreamers, and these kinds of rumors put me into lots of trouble from the more solid and down-to-earth citizen, who care about business much more than about poetry and romance. Even the aesthetic people hound my every step, similarly to the way they used to pursue doctors and scientists in the times of Johann Georg, doing their best to spoil whatever modest existence I strive to maintain. My dear girl, even though I care about your and young Edmund Lehsen's happiness, and will always come to your rescue like a regular *deux ex machina*, I must point out that there will be plenty of people who will never be able to bring themselves to believe that I ever really existed at all. For the benefit of these people, I never present myself as Leonard Turnhäuser, the goldsmith from the sixteenth century. I am quite content with being known merely as a learned man and I encourage everyone to seek explanations of the magic I perform in Wieglieb's 'Natural Magic,' or some other book of this kind. Yet, I have still one more feat to perform, which neither Philidor, nor Philadelphia, nor Cagliostro, nor any other conjurer would ever be able to achieve, and which, being completely inexplicable, must always remain a stumbling block to the kind of people in question. But I must perform it anyway, for it is essential for the conclusion of our Berlin adventure, involving the choosing of the bride by three suitors, the contenders for the hand of the beautiful Fraulein Albertina Fosswinkel. So, do not despair, my dear child. Get up early tomorrow morning, put on your best dress, arrange your hair into your favorite style, and then wait patiently for what is going to happen."

He disappeared exactly as he had come.

At precisely eleven o'clock on Sunday – the appointed hour – old Manasseh with his hopeful nephew, the chancery clerk Tussmann, and Edmund Lehsen with the goldsmith, all arrived at Fosswinkel's house. The suitors, even Baron Benjamin, were all amazed when they saw Albertina, who had never seemed so lovely and becoming. Every lady, married or otherwise, who attaches the proper amount of importance to dress – and you can hardly find one who doesn't, in the entire Berlin – can believe me when I say that Albertina's dress, tailored with extra elegance, was of exactly the right length to show off her pretty little feet in white satin slippers; that its short sleeves and corsage were bordered with very expensive lace; that the distance between the bottom of her sleeves and the top of her white silk gloves, ending just above the elbow, bared a length of her beautiful arms in the most tantalizing way; that her dark, lush hair were decorated with no more than a single gold comb set with jewels, so that the mere addition of a myrtle wreath would be enough to turn this outfit into a wedding gown. But it must be assumed that the true reason she seemed even more beautiful was that love and hope shone in her eyes, and that her cheeks bloomed with excitement.

Fosswinkel, in a burst of hospitality, offered his guests a light brunch. Old Manasseh glowered at the fully laid table with suspicion, but the Baron was less conscientious, for he ate more beefsteak than was seemly, and talked a great deal of stupid nonsense, as was his wont.

The commission councilor behaved wholly contrarily to his nature on this important occasion. Not only did he apparently disregard all thoughts of expense as he poured out bumpers of Port and Madeira, he even offered his guests the hundred year old Malaga from his cellar. At the end of the meal, he explained his decision about the procedure of choosing the future husband for his daughter in a speech much better put together than anybody would have ever expected of him. The suitors were given to understand most clearly that the successful one must find her portrait in the chest of his choice.

At the last stroke of twelve, the door to the hall opened to reveal a table in its center, covered with a rich tapestry, bearing three small chests.

One chest was made of pale gold, with a circle of glittering ducats on its lid, and an inscription inside the circle that read:

"Who chooses me will gain that which he most desires."

The second chest was made of delicately crafted sliver. On its lid, words and letters of foreign languages encircled the inscription:

"Who chooses me will find that which he dares not hope for."

The inscription on the third chest, artfully carved of ivory, read:

"Who chooses me will gain his dreamed-of bliss."

Albertina took her place in a chair behind the table, her father by her side. Manasseh and the goldsmith stepped away into the corner of the room.

The lots were drawn. Tussmann had the first choice, while the Baron and Edmund retreated into the other room.

The chancery clerk stopped thoughtfully in front of the table, looking at the chests, reading and re-reading the inscriptions. Soon he found himself irresistibly attracted by the beautiful foreign letters, twining around so artfully on the cover of the silver chest.

"Good heavens," he exclaimed, "what beautiful lettering, what skill in arranging Arabic characters among the Roman letters. And the inscription! '*Who chooses me will find that which he dares not hope for.*' Haven't I felt all along that I dare not hope that Fraulein Albertina would be so gracious as to honor me with her hand? Haven't I despaired over it? I even tried to throw myself into the pond... Yes, this is where I will find comfort and happiness. Commission councilor, Fraulein Albertina, I choose the silver chest."

Albertina rose and handed him a little key, which he immediately used to open the chest. Great was his shock when he found inside it not Albertina's portrait, but a small parchment-bound book, which, when he opened it, appeared to consist of blank white pages. Beside it lay a little piece of paper that read:

Your wildest hopes you have attained,
A priceless treasure you've obtained.
The gift you find within this cover
You dared not hope for to discover.
Leave *ignorantiam* behind,
Light *sapientiam* in your mind.

"Good heavens," cried Tussmann, "it's a book. Not a book, even – merely paper, bound up together. My hopes are shattered. All is over for me now. All I have got to do is to be off to the frog pond as quickly as I can."

He was about to leave when the goldsmith blocked his way and said:

"Tussmann, don't be foolish. The treasure you acquired is the most precious thing a man like you could possibly have. This verse should have told you so at once. Do me a favor, put this little book into your pocket."

Tussmann did so.

"Now," said the goldsmith, "think of a book you wish you had with you at this moment."

"Oh, my goodness," said Tussmann, "because of my criminal carelessness I went on and drowned Thomasius's treatise on 'Diplomatic Acumen' in the frog pond, like an utter fool that I was."

"Put your hand in your pocket," said the goldsmith, "and take out the book."

Tussmann did so, and lo, the book which he brought out was none other than Thomasius's treatise.

"Ha!" cried Tussmann, "what is this? Why, it is Thomasius's treatise, my beloved Thomasius, rescued from the congregation of frogs in the pond, who would never have learned diplomatic acumen from him."

"Calm down," the goldsmith said; "put the book into your pocket again."

Tussmann did so.

"Now, think of some rare book," the goldsmith said. "Perhaps one you've tried to track down for years but have never been able to find in any library."

"Well," said Tussmann. "Let's see. I do enjoy the opera, and I have always wanted to learn more about the theory of music. I have been trying in vain to get hold of a copy of a certain little treatise which explains the arts of the composer and the performer, in an allegorical form. I am speaking of Johann Beer's 'Musical War', an account of the contest between composition and harmony, which are represented under the guise of two heroines, who battle with each other, and end up completely reconciled."

"Feel in your pocket," said the goldsmith; and the chancery clerk shouted with joy when he found that his book now consisted of Johann Beer's "Musical War".

"You see now, do you not," said the goldsmith, "that in the book which you found in the chest you possess the finest and most complete library that anybody ever had? And more than that, you can always carry it with you. For as long as you have this small volume in your pocket, it will always become whatever book you happen to want to read as soon as you take it out."

Without wasting a thought on Albertina or the commission councilor, Tussmann rushed toward an armchair in the corner, stuck the book into his pocket, pulled it out again, and settled down to read. It was obvious by the delight in his face how completely the goldsmith's promise had been fulfilled.

It was the Baron's turn next. He swaggered up to the table, looked down at the chests through his monocle, and murmured out the inscriptions one after the other. Soon a natural, inborn, irresistible instinct drew him to the gold chest, with the shining ducats on its lid.

"'*Who chooses me will gain that which he most desires*'. Certainly ducats are what I most desire, and Albertina is what I most desire. I don't see much good in bothering over this choice any longer."

He grasped the golden chest, took its key from Albertina, and opened it.

Inside was a neat metal file. Beside it lay a piece of paper with the words:

With this choice you have acquired
That which you have most desired.
From now on your trade will strive,
Moving on with utmost drive,
For as long as you're alive.

"What the Devil's the use of this thing?" Benjie cried, surveying the file. "It isn't Albertina's picture. The only use for this chest is to take it and present it to Albertina as a wedding present. Come to me, my beauty..."

With these words, he headed straight for Albertina, but the goldsmith held him back by the shoulder and said:

"Stop, my good sir; this is not our agreement. You must content yourself with the file. And you will be content with it, when you find out what a treasure it is. In fact, the poem should have already told you what it is. Do you happen to have a worn golden ducat in your pocket?"

"I do," said Benjie irritably. "So what?"

"Take it out," the Goldsmith said, "and try the file on the edge of it."

The Baron did so, with an amount of skill which told of much previous practice. Remarkably, the ducat not only didn't get smaller with the filing, but appear to grow until it looked brand new. The same happened with the second and the third ducat. In fact, the more Benjie filed the ducats, the better they became.

Up to this point Manasseh had been looking on in silence. But suddenly he jumped up, his eyes sparkling wildly, and dashed at his nephew, crying, in a hollow, terrible voice:

"God of my fathers! What do I see? Give me that file! – Give it to me instantly! It's magical. This is the very item, for which I sold my soul to the Devil more than three hundred years ago. God of my fathers... hand it over to me!"

He grasped at the file, but Benjie pushed him back, crying:

"Get away, you old idiot! It was I who found the file, not you!"

Manasseh rushed at him in fury:

"Viper! Worm-eaten fruit of my race! – Give me the file! All the demons of Hell be upon you, accursed thief!"

Manasseh clutched the Baron with a torrent of curses, foaming and gnashing his teeth, trying with all his might to wrestle the file away. But Benjie fought for it with the fury of a lioness defending her cubs. At length, old Manasseh was worn out, and his nephew seized him by the shoulders with bone-crushing force and threw him out of the door. He then dashed back like a flash of lightning, set a small table into a corner of the room opposite to the chancery clerk, took a handful of ducats from his pocket, and started filing them as hard as he could.

"Now," said the goldsmith, "we have finally rid ourselves of old Manasseh. Rumors have it that he is the second Ahasuerus, and has been haunting this world since 1572. Back then he was knowns as Lippold the coiner, burned at the stake for diabolical practices and sorcery. It is said that the Devil saved his body from death in exchange for his immortal soul. Even though Lippold is rumored to be able to change his appearance, some of the learned people have recognized him here in Berlin. This is how the legend was born that in our times not one, but many Lippolds wander the world. It is good that my knowledge of magic enabled me to expel him for good."

It would weary you needlessly, dear

reader, if I were to waste words on telling you what you already know quite well: that Edmund Lehsen was left with the only choice of the ivory chest, inscribed: "*Who chooses me will gain his dreamed-of bliss*", and found inside it a beautiful miniature portrait of Albertina, along with the following poem:

You have earned the highest prize
Meet your darling's loving eyes.
Unhappy days are left behind,
No more rejection will you find.
Embrace the long-desired bliss
By meeting your beloved's kiss.

And Edmund, like Bassanio, followed this advice of the last line by pressing his blushing sweetheart to his chest and kissing her on the lips. The commission councilor was beside himself with joy at the happy conclusion of such an eventful courtship of his daughter.

Meanwhile the Baron had been filing ducats as eagerly and absorbedly as the chancery clerk had been reading. Neither of them took the slightest notice of what had been going on, until the commission councilor announced that Edmund Lehsen had chosen the chest containing Albertina's portrait, and was, consequently, to be her husband. Tussmann seemed to be quite delighted to hear it, and expressed his satisfaction in his usual manner, by rubbing his hands, jumping up and down for a moment or two, and giving a delicate little laugh. The Baron seemed to feel no further interest in the matter, but he embraced the commission councilor and thanked him for being a real gentleman who had made him most utterly happy by his present of the magical file, and who, from now on, could always count on the Baron's support in all his affairs. With this, he took his rapid departure.

Tussmann, too, thanked the commission councilor with tears in his eyes for making him the happiest of men by giving him this most rare and wonderful of all the rare and wonderful books; and, after the most profuse flood of compliments to Albertina, Edmund, and the old goldsmith, he followed the Baron out the door.

From now on, the Baron Benjie ceased to torture the world with his literary exploits, and spent all his time filing ducats. Tussmann no longer made the booksellers' lives a burden by pestering them with his perpetual hunts for old forgotten books.

After a few weeks of rapture and

happiness, the commission councilor's house sank into sadness, for the goldsmith urged Edmund to keep his solemn promise and depart for Italy.

Although parting with Albertina was painful for Edmund, he also felt the urge to visit the motherland of all arts. And Albertina, while shedding bitter tears at the thought of parting with her love, could not help thinking how much attention she would get by taking letters from Italy out of her work basket during the aesthetic tea parties she frequented.

Edmund has been in Rome for more than a year, and people say that his letters to Albertina are becoming rarer, and that her responses are not quite as passionate as before. Who knows, maybe even their engagement will eventually break off? Certainly Albertina will not remain unmarried for long; she is so pretty, and so well off. Besides, there is a rumor that young Herr Gloksin, a court clerk and a very comely young gentleman with a slim, tightly girded waist, double waistcoat, and a cravat tied in the English style, has been Albertina Fosswinkel's dance partner at all the winter balls and often accompanies her to the Thiergarten, while the commission councilor trots very happily after them, looking like a satisfied father. Moreover, Herr Gloksin has just passed his second judge examination with excellent marks, as admitted by all the examiners who had been drilling him since morning like a decayed tooth. The very fact of this examination hints at the idea that the court clerk is harboring thoughts of marriage as soon as he can accomplish a significant advance in his career.

It is quite possible that Albertina may consider marrying the court clerk, once he achieves a high position in the society. Let us see what happens.

www.ingramcontent.com/pod-product-compliance
Lightning Source LLC
Chambersburg PA
CBHW020330030826
48979CB00021B/521

* 9 7 8 1 9 4 0 0 7 6 4 6 1 *